THE TRIALS OF

ARCADIA

-

'If you don't know where you are going any road can take you there'

Lewis Carroll

-

Alice Kilian

COPYRIGHT

Alice Kilian

'The Trials of Arcadia'

© 2021, Alice Kilian

Self-published

(aliceuk200@gmail.com)

All rights reserved.

ISBN: 9798751890131

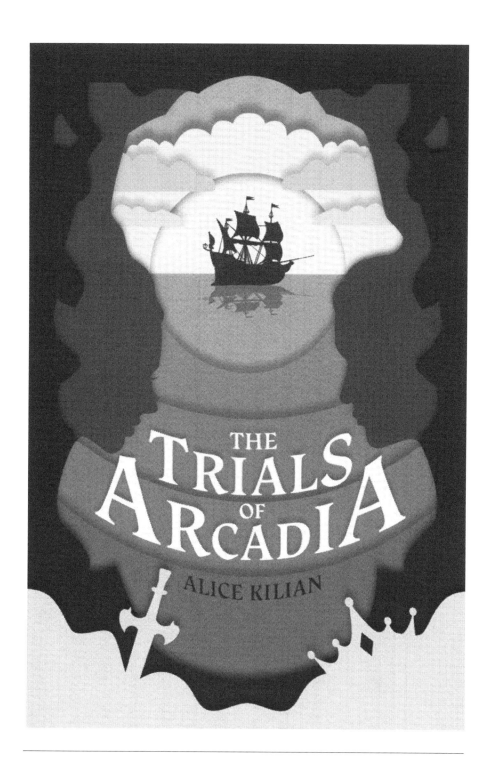

THE TRIALS OF ARCADIA

ALICE KILIAN

ABOUT THE AUTHOR

Alice Kilian is a 20-year-old first time author who grew up in Gosport, Hampshire. Alice has always been a creative person and loves to read all sorts of books. Her favourite books include 'Harry Potter', 'The Chronicles of Narnia', 'Percy Jackson' and 'Private Peaceful'. At secondary school, Alice began writing short stories, and these soon turned to longer, more in depth works. 'The Trials of Arcadia' has been an ongoing project for Alice and she hopes to release two more books to complete the trilogy. Alice wrote her debut novel whilst stuck at home during the national lockdowns of the pandemic. Alice has expressed interest in writing other books set in Arcadia, though she currently has no plans to write them until after university.

TO

MARGOT

-

'My cat, who sat on my lap during the whole of lockdown

and helped me write.'

PROLOGUE

There was a time when the Arcadians roamed the Earth, celestial beings who harboured great power and rich culture. Their home, the city of Arcadia, stood proudly overlooking the vast valley of Arivale. Arivale was a peaceful land, home to a high elvish race called the Grigori. Magic grew throughout the valley, flowing through the veins of every living thing, but good things never last.

In the early hours of a summer morning, when the valley was slowly waking from a peaceful sleep, the earth began to tremble. At first it was soft, like a slight wind might ripple a body of water, but it became a wild tree-felling wind in a matter of minutes. As the earth shook, the Grigori tribes were displaced. Some were swallowed by the creeping crack that spread across the valley and many died in their beds, heads resting against soft pillows that would now comfort them forever. The quake lasted no more than five minutes, yet the devastation caused was haunting.

A young magician named Eemos, who had been passing through the valley at the time of the earthquake, saw the ruins of the once-great city and offered his assistance. He promised safe passage and welcomed refugees to venture east to his homeland where he assured them, they would be welcomed.

In this matter, the six tribes were divided. Many were cautious of travelling so far east and others welcomed the change, calling it an opportunity from the Gods. Four of the six tribes gathered what was left of their belongings and accepted Eemos's offer. They were Kiba, Kelasso, Nixam and Shaman. The two remaining tribes, Delos and Venator, were set in their ways and too proud to accept help. Delos, especially, held themselves in great esteem.

As the travellers began their journey east, they looked back at the crumbling ruins of their homes, and the loved ones they were leaving behind. For many weeks they travelled in harsh conditions, across rocky terrain and through scorching deserts until, exhausted, the Grigori were ready to lose hope of the promise of sanctuary.

High above them on a steep sand dune, Eemos stopped and turned to face them. 'Welcome to Osaria,' he smiled.

As they rushed forward and reached the peak of a dune, the

Grigori saw a vast land that stretched from their feet to the horizon. The bustling expanse that lay before them was alive with colour as hundreds of figures below moved like sand on the wind.

They went about their daily lives, some working at fresh fruit stands while others hammered away at iron in their workshops. Children played in the water of a huge reservoir in the centre of the settlement. An enormous pavilion stood at the far side of the water. It was draped in fabrics of all different colours and towered over the other much smaller tents. As promised, the Grigori were welcomed with open arms, accepted by the eastern magicians, known as the Magi.

The Magi's abilities were astounding, like nothing the Grigori had ever seen before. In the evenings, around a large fire by the pavilion, the Grigori gathered to watch the Magi display their magical talents making the fire dance and the water climb high up into the air before crashing back down with such might.

The Grigori too had magical powers, though theirs were more spiritual. Each kind of magic was divided amongst the tribes, the elders teaching others how to master those powers. Delos for instance were accustomed to ice magic, while Kiba were healers, who practiced the magic of the earth.

One particular form of magic that interested the Grigori was the portals cast by the Magi that could transport you from place to place. They were called Orbs, small cylindrical marbles that contained coloured, glowing liquids. Only a few of the Magi had these strange objects, but they were always kept close, on a pendant or the hilt of a sword. Such curious objects were clearly of great value as one of the Magi was overheard telling another about Reapers from the south who sought orbs to sell to the highest bidder.

Reapers had been spotted near Arivale before, though they dare not attack due to the military force of the Venator tribe, the defenders and guards of the city. Reapers were foul goblin-like creatures, obsessed with wealth and power. The Magi seemed well prepared for any attack. They certainly had the numbers to defend themselves, though the Grigori felt unsettled as their own military force hadn't journeyed east with them.

As the years drifted by and the Grigori settled in their new home, nerves calmed, with many joining smaller Magi parties as they journeyed throughout the lands. They took the collective name of travellers, and some say small groups of them are still around today, still practicing their magic and still as fierce. You might even be able to find them if you know where to look.

CHAPTER 1

HIGHSHORE

The sheets were damp when Danny woke up. The brittle single paned glass of his window offered no protection from the elements. His shoulders were sore from the cold and the chilling air burned his opening eyes. The sun shone through the window, dancing like fire along the peeling white walls. The light hit the pillow beside him, inching closer and closer to his face. He tried to escape the day creeping towards him, but it was no use. Sitting up, he stretched his legs down to meet the harsh wooden floor.

The first of the early morning traders were stirring in the streets below, each raring to get the best spot to sell their goods. The bells rang out, echoing between the tightly knit thatched houses. No doubt by this time ships were already flooding into the docks, which meant more customers for the stalls and the taverns. Danny grabbed his crumpled clothes from the chair at his desk. After dressing, he adjusted his hair in a small circular mirror mounted on the wall by the door. He smiled at his reflection, before being rudely interrupted by a chiming bell below. He swiftly left the room, grabbing his belt and bag from the hook on his door. As the heavy wooden door shut against the delicate frame, the walls shook, causing the mirror to fall and smash on the floor.

As he leapt down the winding stairs, the milk cart rode past. Danny chased after it, only just catching up in time to jump into the passenger seat before it descended the steep stone cobbles of Primrose Hill.

'Morning, Danny,' the milkman chuckled. 'For a minute there I thought you weren't gonna make it.'

'I overslept, Simon. Luckily the bells reminded me,' he smiled.

The cart rode straight down the hill every morning, carrying Danny to Avery docks. He was allowed to ride on the condition that he helped old Si with the milk deliveries. They were almost there. Mrs Carson at number four as well as Mr Rogers at number six were all that were left. These, Si could do by himself, and besides, the docks and Danny's market stall were only a short walk from here.

He had worked as a fishmonger's assistant for two years, since he was fourteen. His father had gotten him the job before joining the Navy. Soon after, he had left for the shores of a distant land, and Danny hadn't seen him since. Danny didn't mind living alone—in fact he quite liked it—but life was repetitive and dull, especially working for the fishmonger, Oliver.

Oliver was a snide man. He cheated people out of their money at work as well as at the gambling tables. He was light fingered too, something he'd taught Danny and the other children who would play on the street. Admittedly this had helped Danny through some difficult times, but he didn't have to steal anymore. A year or so ago he had begun to receive cheques from an anonymous benefactor, which allowed him to rent his lodgings and pay his way. Sometimes, Danny wished he could leave his work at Oliver's, but he knew the money wouldn't last. It wasn't all bad though. He knew all the regular customers and managed to trade a few of his own catches on the side, to clients he knew were looking for something special. Of course, Oliver knew nothing about this. He could never know.

A few years back, Danny had found a small cove with shallow waters and huge rock pools, with intricate tunnels and passages through the water. It was a haven for fish and yet no one except Danny had ever found it. With tons of rainbow fish and carp galore, it was these warm pools that Danny was thinking of when he reached the market.

The marketplace was always lively, and Danny got to work immediately. First, he helped Oliver unload some fresh catches from the barrels, then he went down to the docks to collect their morning delivery from the fisherman. He noticed a huge ship with great black sails anchored not far offshore. It was odd for a ship to come so close to the port, but not to dock, unless it had nothing to trade. If that was the case though, why had it come to Highshore?

Danny finished his errands and headed back to the market. It was about twelve noon when Danny's day finally began to get interesting. Whilst daydreaming at his stall, Danny's eye was caught by a beautiful young woman. She stood with great posture on the far side of the market, her dark red dress blowing freely in the wind. Her thick black hair was plaited down to the small of her back and she wore heavy duty lace up boots. As she turned, Danny caught sight of her face. Rosy cheeks and velvety red lips greeted him. She met his eye from across the market and seemed to study his face. She whispered something to her chaperones, two men who seemed much older than she was. They looked rough, with cuts and scars covering their bare arms. They did not match her poised demeanour in the slightest. Danny watched as they walked towards him. The girl stopped at a nearby merchant's stand, to look at silks and dresses from the Far East. He watched as she stroked the fabric between her fingers and then pressed it against her cheek. Danny was mesmerised. She looked across the courtyard at Danny, but quickly turned away. Moving ever closer, this time stopping at a table full of trinkets, she lifted a shiny gold cup and held it up to the light. The rays of golden sun shone from the chalice onto her face as she inspected the curious object. She tilted her head playfully, once again glancing at Danny, who sat up in his chair. He was infatuated with her. As they finally reached his stall Danny cleared his throat in readiness to introduce himself.

'Lovely day, isn't it Miss?' Danny said, as he stepped forwards.

She smiled and said softly, 'I was wondering if you might give me directions to The Navigator? I believe it's the best inn around these parts.'

'Of course,' he grinned enthusiastically. 'It's just down that road, on the right.'

She looked at him inquisitively.

'Forgive me, but I can't help wondering why a strong young man like yourself is stuck working in a market?' She shook her head. 'Sorry, it's not my place to say, but you look bored, like you could do with an adventure?'

'Well...I...' Danny laughed, her questions throwing him off guard. 'I do usually go on many urrm... adventures,' he lied, trying to impress her.

'Oh really?' She lifted her eyes to meet his. "So, this job is…temporary?'

'I'm on a break at the moment, actually,' Danny lied again, rubbing the back of his neck, hoping she would believe him.

'Well, if you fancy another adventure,' she replied. 'I'll be at The Navigator. Just ask for Isabelle.'

Danny smiled with the corner of his mouth. 'I'll be sure to swing by, don't you worry.'

A loud whistle blew, interrupting their conversation. Danny turned to see a red-headed girl sprint into the marketplace. She knocked over the mannequin at the fabric stand, tripped, pulled the tablecloth off the trinket stall and sent cups, statues and all kinds of artefacts flying into the air. They clattered to the floor with a tremendous crash echoing around the square.

Rushing after the careless girl were three scary looking men dressed in black. They shouted after her, causing even more of a scene in the marketplace. Danny turned back to face Isabelle, but she had disappeared into the crowd as the men quickly cornered the girl in front of the fish stand.

Danny leapt over the counter, knowing that if Oliver's fish were to go flying too, he would never be forgiven. The men edged closer as the girl backed right up to Danny, who was guarding the fish with his life. She bumped into him, gasped and turned. Her face was covered in dirt, it was the first thing Danny noticed. The second was that he recognised her. They had gone to the same school and although she'd been a year or two below Danny, he recognised her fiery auburn hair and scruffy appearance.

'Keira?' he asked. The men were still shouting and now had an audience.

Danny didn't know if she heard him or if she was ignoring him. Either way he was sure that it was her.

'You little wretch,' one of the men growled.

'This girl—!' He faced the gathering crowd as they edged forward, not wanting to miss the excitement. '—crept into the cellar of the Drunken Sailor and tried to steal from our safe!'

The crowd was maybe ten people strong, and they were all staring at the girl.

Moving alongside Danny, her voice sang out, 'I would never…' there was a sweetness in her tone which Danny found strangely captivating, especially given the circumstances. 'I would never have done such a thing. I was just looking for the bathroom when I stumbled upon an unlocked safe. I was about to call for the owner, but before I could they all came down the stairs and accused me.'

Danny didn't believe her story, but nor did he want her to be arrested or beaten up by these men.

'Now that you mention it,' Danny perked up, 'they hardly ever lock that bottom room, and the bathrooms are difficult to find.'

Some of the crowd nodded in agreement as Keira looked at Danny thankfully. 'He's right, and when they started chasing me, I had no choice but to run.'

The tallest and roughest of the men grunted under his breath. He knew he had no evidence to arrest the girl and the last thing he wanted was to lose business over quarrelling with a child.

'Stay away from our pub or next time you might not be so lucky,' he growled, then reluctantly pushed through the spectators, leaving her with Danny.

The crowd, disappointed that the excitement was over, dispersed and went about their otherwise dull day.

Danny looked around the market to see if Isabel was still around, but alas she and her companions had left with the rest.

Disappointed, he turned to face Keira. 'So go on then, what happened?' he asked, looking questioningly at her.

'Don't worry about it,' she replied.

'Look, all I'm worried about is keeping this stall standing. Some of the others weren't so lucky,' he said, gesturing to the carnage strewn around the floor.

'I know what you're thinking,' she snapped fiercely. 'You think that I'm a thief and that I'm dirty and poor and you're judging me. But you don't know me. You know nothing about me.'

As she turned to walk away, Danny grabbed her arm. 'What I

think,' he said, 'is that you're a good liar and—' He lifted the satchel from her shoulder, opening it before she had a chance to object. He revealed an array of gold pieces. '—you're clearly good at what you do.'

Keira lunged at Danny, trying to snatch her bag back, but he was too quick. He stepped back, holding the bag high above his head, laughing as she jumped up trying to reach the bag.

'Give it back,' she cried, falling short of the mark.

Danny laughed again. 'You'll have to try harder than that, I thought you were a good thief.'

With that, she punched Danny in the stomach, making him double over in pain.

'Thank you,' she grinned as she plucked the bag from his hand. 'And thank you for earlier too.' Her tone was more reluctant this time before she turned away and hurried out of the marketplace, disappearing down a dark alley.

'You're welcome!' Danny shouted after her as he regained his composure and returned to his full height.

CHAPTER 2

THE NAVIGATOR

As six o'clock came and went and the market grew quiet, Danny noticed the large tatty ship was still anchored offshore. He wondered what kind of people crewed a ship so old and rugged. Perhaps they were merchants from a faraway land that had used this same ship on many adventures to travel all over the world. They could have come to Highshore to restock on supplies and take time off from travelling. Or perhaps they were traders from the south where the scorching sun had aged the dark wood.

As far as he could tell, there was nothing wrong with the frame of the ship. The three masts stood tall and strong, as if they were grand. A bright golden statue attached to the bow glinted like a beacon in the setting sun. Her arms were flung back, her hair flowing freely behind her as if shaped by the wind. All that was needed, thought Danny, was a good lick of paint, a couple of new sails and she'd be truly grand.

Turning back to his stall, Danny looked up and down at the empty crates. Completely sold out, he decided he was ready to go home. Oliver was nowhere to be seen and had probably found his way down to the tavern. Not the Drunken Sailor of course. He had been banned from that place years ago. With a sigh, Danny packed up the empty crates, loaded them into the back of Oliver's cart, locked it shut for the next day and set off to find his boss, who had a habit of getting himself into trouble when he had been drinking. No doubt he would suffer the consequences of Oliver's bad mood the next day if anything were to happen.

Danny reckoned The Navigator was Oliver's likely destination. It had a back room often used by sailors to gamble away their fortunes, something Danny knew Oliver couldn't resist even though he had little luck and even less coin to pay his way.

This of course was not the only reason that Danny wanted to go. The Navigator was the Inn where Isabelle was staying and, fancying himself as a bit of a ladies' man, Danny planned to find her. This time he needed to really impress her as he doubted that she had believed his last story.

The truth was, Danny had little practice with a sword. Years ago, his father had taught him to fight with wooden poles, and Danny was quite good for his age. But that was years ago, and his dull everyday life had gotten in the way of hobbies. Besides, what use was sword fighting to a fishmonger? His father had only allowed him to hold a real sword once, but it had been much too heavy for him. He wondered what had become of his father, all these years with no contact, with only vague memories of him left. Danny wished his lies were true. He wanted to be a strong, brave man like his father had been. Instead, he sold fish, day in and day out. He didn't want to end up like Oliver. This wasn't his forever job, it couldn't be. He thought about Isabelle's words, the way she had said that he needed an adventure. He hoped to see her again and find out more about her offer.

The Navigator was usually a fairly quiet spot, but tonight was different. Danny had never seen it so full. The saloon had a low ceiling with dark wooden beams running its length. It was dingy, the only natural light coming from a small round window at the front of the building. The rest of the room was lit by lanterns, which provided a shabby ambience.

The customers were not the familiar patrons that Danny was used to. This was odd as Danny knew almost everyone in Highshore and this evening he recognised very few faces. They must have sailed in this morning, Danny thought. He could see they were a rugged bunch, all with swords hanging from their waists. Some had cuts and bruises, others were missing limbs. Danny noticed peg legs and eye patches dotted around the room. Most were filthy with thick layers of dirt on their faces, but all were enjoying themselves and seemed too drunk to do much harm. That being said, Danny would bet money that these men could fight, drunk or not.

There were around twenty of them in the main bar and when Danny reached the back room, he saw a half a dozen more. As he entered, he pulled a red velvet curtain aside to reveal the crowd. These men and women were better dressed, less dirty and had significantly more limbs than the others. They were playing cards. Blackjack, Danny could see. All but one of the players looked up.

At the head of the table, face hidden by an enormous black hat, sat a man dressed in fine silks and bedazzled with jewels. He didn't seem to care that Danny had interrupted the game. He was clearly in charge here, the captain perhaps? As he lifted his head slowly, his face became clear. It wasn't the sort of face you'd want to look at for too long, his piercing eyes would scare you away. He was middle aged, though he looked older due to a jagged scar that stretched down the left side of his face. His skin was tattered and cracked. He had long greasy black hair, braided with all sorts of shiny metals. His beard matched, though it was not as dark as his midnight locks. Streaks of grey ran though it like clouds in the sky. Danny looked away. He felt nervous and knew that he didn't belong here. Sat to the Captain's left, staring at him intently, was Isabelle, with a soft smile upon her lips. Without taking her eyes off him, she leaned over and whispered something into the captain's ear. Slowly, he looked up at Danny.

'Is this the one?' he muttered to her.

She nodded.

'What do you want, boy?' his gravelly voice bellowed out across the room.

'I-I um,' Danny stammered, then composed himself. 'Nothing, I was just looking for someone.' He scanned the room for any signs of Oliver, but he was nowhere to be seen.

'Sit!' the captain commanded.

One of the men drew up a chair and gestured for Danny to take a seat.

He did as he was told. So much for speaking to Isabelle alone, he thought.

'He doesn't look like much,' the captain snarled. 'No more than a boy.'

The crew laughed.

'My Isabelle tells me you're in need of adventure. She thinks that you should join us and become a pirate.'

'What? Well, I…'

'I think she's wrong,' the captain looked him up and down. 'You wouldn't last a week.'

Danny didn't know what to say to this, so he kept quiet.

'Out! the captain roared. 'He has nothing to offer us.'

Danny was hauled to his feet and bundled out of the room. Confused and hurt by the captain's words, he looked back as the curtain fell and saw Isabelle once again whisper something into the captain's ear.

'Are you sure about this one?" The captain looked doubtingly at Isabelle.

'Oh yes,' said Isabelle confidently. 'He's the one I saw in my vision.'

CHAPTER 3

THE HELLBOURNE PRINCESS

Danny didn't sleep a wink. His wild thoughts controlled the night. He thought of Isabelle, her soft smile and curious eyes. He thought of the captain's harsh tone and unforgiving demeanour. Danny wondered what life at sea was like, if the pirates had explored the world, and what kinds of things they might have seen. He had heard stories, myths and legends about faraway lands and extraordinary creatures. But were they just that, myths?

He tossed and turned in his bed, running through thousands of different scenarios in his mind. The next morning Danny rose earlier than usual, bored of a sleepless night. Packing a leather satchel with a few old books, his fishing equipment and a sandwich, he headed off down to the hidden cove so that he could read, bask in the sunshine and maybe catch a fish or two before work. As he walked, his mind wandered.

Halfway down Primrose Hill he could just about make out the looming shape of the great wooden ship floating gently on the waves.

As he reached the market and turned right towards the beach, Danny was disturbed by a loud crash. Turning towards the noise, he saw a cat run out from behind some old crates and shoot down the road in front of him. With a shrug he continued on towards the end of the road. A few moments later he heard faint voices behind him, followed by footsteps approaching rapidly.

He turned to see three men running towards him. Instinctively he sprinted away, darting down the next street and hoping they wouldn't follow. They were rough and rugged, and he recognised one of them from the Navigator. Were they chasing him? The answer to that came soon enough. The men followed him down the alley. He tried to run further but realised it was a dead end. He was trapped. One of the men grabbed him by the shoulders, spun him round and bound his hands while another tied cloth over his eyes. He began to shout but was quickly gagged. He kicked and wriggled and felt his body being lifted from the floor. He was being carried over someone's shoulder. Someone big. He gave up the struggle and lay still for a while, trying to figure out where he was being taken. Believe it or not, this was not the first time Danny had been kidnapped. Once when Oliver had bet money, he didn't have on a poker game he didn't win, Danny had been used as collateral and forced to run errands for a local gangster. This time, he suspected, it had nothing to do with Oliver.

The men stayed silent, and all Danny could hear were their footsteps and the birds. He could tell by the sound of gulls that they were near the sea and by the smell he guessed they were in or still near the market. This was confirmed when he heard Oliver's smug voice bragging about his victory at the card tables the night before. Danny tried to shout, but it came out as a muffled cry and was much too quiet for Oliver to hear. Danny wondered if Oliver would have done anything even if he had seen him being manhandled. He doubted it. Oliver considered himself to be much too precious and wouldn't have fought over anything that didn't benefit him. Danny wondered how long it would take Oliver to replace him at the fish stand should these thugs wring his neck. There were plenty of street kids who would die to have his job. His thoughts wandered so much that he had almost forgotten about his current predicament.

They had passed the market now and Danny could feel that they were no longer walking on solid ground. They must be on a pontoon or dock, he thought. He felt the ground change again as his carrier stepped onto an even wobblier surface. What with that and the sound of waves lapping against a wooden surface, it was obvious they were on a boat.

The man carrying him threw him down as easily as he had slung him over his shoulder and while the restraints around his wrists were still tight, the cloth covering his eyes was slipping.

By moving his head up and down, the fabric loosened further still until his eyes were free of the damp and dirty cloth. From the front of the boat, Danny watched as Primrose Hill and Avery docks slowly drifted away.

Danny turned to face his kidnappers. In front of him sat two men, rowing with all their strength against the tide. He was wedged between the wooden sides and the knees of the rowers. A larger man, who he assumed was his carrier, was sitting at the rear of the tiny rowing boat, weighing down the back and lifting the front clear out of the water. Focusing his attention on his mouth restraint, Danny stretched his neck and wiggled his jaw from side to side in a very unflattering manner until eventually the gag came loose. He spat it onto the floor of the boat along with some stray bits of fluff that were now stuck to his tongue.

The men didn't seem to care that Danny was slowly freeing himself from his bonds. This was probably the least of their worries. With the shore so far away, where would he go even if he did manage to free his hands? Shuffling in his seat, Danny turned instead to see where they were going. No surprise, they were beelining straight towards the tatty pirate ship and although he prayed that they would pass it by, he knew this was not the case. As they neared the ship, Danny could read the chipped golden lettering at its bow. 'The Hellbourne Princess,' he spoke aloud.

'She's the finest ship outside the King's Navy.' The big man grinned, showing off his yellow and black teeth.

'Really?' Danny said, unconvinced as he studied the outside of the ship more closely.

Up close, the ship looked far from majestic. More like a wreck, thought Danny, although he kept that opinion to himself. Its tattered sails and dodgy paint job weren't the only things wrong with it. One of the three masts was badly split and there were numerous holes in the sides, where cannonballs had ripped through the aged wood.

'So, you're pirates then?' he asked one of the rowers, trying to make a little light-hearted conversation.

'Quiet, lad!' he snapped.

So much for that plan, thought Danny as he looked back to the large man at the stern of the boat. He sat quietly fiddling with something in his jacket, looking up at Danny as a small furry head peeked out of his top pocket.

'It's a ferret,' he said, noticing Danny's gaze as he fed his furry friend a tidbit.

Danny was surprised, but impressed that this huge, scary looking man had managed to keep such a small thing alive. Danny hoped that he hadn't squashed or kicked the poor little fellow during his abduction.

'This is my Meg,' he said, holding her up proudly until she wriggled down his arm and disappeared back into his pocket. 'What's your name, lad?'

'Danny,' he replied. 'And you?'

'Mouse.'

'Mouse,' said Danny. 'What kind of name is that?'

'You've never met anyone called Mouse before?' he asked, looking all confused.

'Can't say that I have,' said Danny.

'Well, I've never met anyone called Danny,' he responded, looking a bit put out. 'My name isn't that strange. You must not have met very many people.'

Danny thought about this for a moment, realising that Mouse was right. He hadn't really met anyone from outside of Highshore before.

'Sorry,' he said, as a rope ladder was thrown down from the deck above.

'Get climbing, lad!' said the rude rower gruffly as he untied Danny's hands.

Danny did as he was told and grabbed hold of the rope. Covered in slime and soaking from the sea spray, Danny held on for dear life as he slowly shimmied up towards the deck. followed by the remaining three passengers of the tugboat. Danny wasn't convinced that the rope would hold him, two hefty rowers, the full weight of Mouse and Meg, but nonetheless he kept climbing. As he reached the top he was greeted by a whole host of people. Some he recognised from the tavern the night before, but many of the faces he saw were new. Danny was surprised at how many of them were on the ship, it was packed on deck and, he guessed, there were probably many more below.

As he looked round for Isabelle, a voice bellowed, 'Fall in, the lot of you!'

As everyone lined up across the centre of the ship, Danny was shoved into line by Mouse, who stood behind him. The deck fell silent, and the voice called again.

'Look alive, crew!' the voice bellowed as its owner marched down the stairs and stepped onto the deck.

Well-built and muscular, she had mountains of dreadlocked hair spilling out from all sides of her dark red bandana. Danny recognised her from the captain's poker game.

'My name is Melanie Lui. For those of you who don't know, I am the First Mate aboard this ship. I know everything that happens on board, so don't think you can get anything past me.'

She wore fitted black trousers and shiny boots. Her oversized cream shirt was wrapped around her waist with a thick leather belt from which her sword hung.

'Right then, new crew members step forward,' she said, her command leaving no room for argument.

Ushered along by Mouse, Danny shuffled forward.

He heard other footsteps pattering around him, but no one dared take their eyes off the First Mate as she glared menacingly at each of them.

Danny wondered if the other newcomers were also from Highshore. Perhaps he'd know some of them, he thought. The First Mate turned and gestured to a group of men guarding the upper deck. They nodded back and opened two large oak doors.

A moment later, the ship's Captain from the night before appeared and gazed down at the crew. Danny looked at the ground, hoping to blend in and not be noticed.

'Captain Gabriel Moreno,' announced the First Mate as the Captain made his way down the stairs slowly.

Perhaps it was for suspense or to scare the newcomers. Either way, it was working. Danny could hear panicked breathing to his left and chattering teeth to his right. Taking a deep breath, he looked up, searching for the owner of the wobbly jaw. It comforted him that he was not the only one scared by the captain's presence. He looked around but before he could find who he was looking for he was met by a familiar face. It was the last face he wanted to see, but the pale freckled face of Keira was oddly comforting. Staring back at him, her red hair glinting in the sun, Danny couldn't believe it. He hadn't seen this annoying girl for years and now twice in two days! And what's more, he was now stuck on board a ship with her for who knows how long. His day was getting better and better.

CHAPTER 4

'OSARIA'

LAND OF THE MAGI & GRIGORI

Quick as a flash, an arrow shot through the air, narrowly missing Elda's head.

Ariadne's bow was poised and ready to fire again. She looked through the leafy trees, trying to catch sight of movement, but Elda had shrunk back into the shadows. A twig snapped to her left. She turned quickly, fired and immediately drew another arrow from her quiver. Not having hit anything, she climbed farther up the tall cedar tree, slinging the bow over her shoulder as she grappled for higher branches. Ariadne found a secure perch overlooking the woods. From here she could see for miles and miles, a sea of tree canopies floating gently in the breeze. Out of the corner of her eye she caught a glimpse of movement. Her lightning-fast reflexes kicked in and within seconds she had released another arrow.

'You've got to do better than that, Princess!' Elda shouted from below.

'Enough with the Princess talk,' came Ariadne's reply.

'Maybe I'll listen, Your Highness, but you'll have to catch me first,' she cried as she sprinted through an opening in the trees, dodging two more arrows as she darted behind a large moss-covered rock.

Ariadne quickly climbed down the tree, trying to stay as quiet as possible. From the low branches she jumped onto the rock.

'Gotcha!' she yelled, pointing her last arrow down to where Elda was standing.

'Not quite,' said Elda as she vanished into thin air, then reappeared behind Ariadne. She whistled tunefully as Ariadne turned to face her. Elda drew her knife. 'I guess I win this time Princess.' She grinned.

'That's not fair! You used magic!' said Ariadne.

'And you used your elven reflexes and your heightened senses, so we're even.'

'Well, that's different, I can't help that.'

'Don't worry, you beat me every other time.'

'That's true, I suppose.' They laughed as a deep brass horn blew in the distance, signalling the end of the game.

They rode towards the walls of the lower town, the morning sun glinting on the domed roof of the golden palace above. Osaria was a truly majestic place, rich in culture and deep in history. There was an ambience that drew all sorts of people towards it, and no one quite knew why. Princess Ariadne had lived in Osaria her whole life. In fact, her family had ruled Osaria for over a century, ever since the great alliance between the Grigori and the Magi.

Ariadne's ancestor, the legendary Eemos of Osaria, had led the largest mass movement of culture in history. This resulted in the Elven people of the Grigori joining the Magicians and forming a single united kingdom, the strongest of its kind in the east for many years.

The descendants of Eemos were well-respected throughout the lands and had numerous allies across Arcadia. Ariadne and her brothers had been invited to visit many of the kingdoms, the rulers hoping their children would marry into the Osarian Royal family.

Ariadne always managed to find an excuse to avoid meeting suitors. She wanted to marry for love and not obligation. She was the youngest of five and, being the only daughter, had always been the apple of her father's eye. Ariadne's eldest brother, Darius, would one day be King. He and his wife Selena would rule Arcadia and eventually their children would rule. The next in line for the throne were her brothers Behnam and Casper followed by Amir, Ariadne's twin and then herself. This meant that she had very few royal duties and could lead a fairly normal life, though her father still expected her to, one day, marry a Prince from a faraway land. She understood that the kingdom needed allies but hated that she was constantly used as a pawn.

Elda, on the other hand, had moved to Osaria when she was six years old and quickly became friends with Ariadne, though her life was not as carefree. Her mother worked in the palace kitchen and Elda served as lady-in-waiting to Ariadne. She was a fullblood Magi, which was quite uncommon, as most of the Osarian citizens were a mixture of Grigori and Magi. Elda's ancestors had been travellers before the Grigori joined the Magi and her family had only recently returned. Her earliest memories had been of great sand dunes and faraway cities. She had loved travelling, but much preferred the security of living in Osaria.

Despite being surrounded by wealth, Elda had little of her own. She helped her mother look after her two younger siblings as well as her responsibilities to Ariadne. She lived a good life, though she couldn't help but want more. She wanted to make something of herself. To be recognised for her own merits. Though she had lived in Osaria for the past ten years, she still felt something of an outsider.

As they reached the gates a group of young men approached them led by Isaac, a tall, strapping centaur with a mass of curly brown hair that rested on his shoulders. Isaac was half horse half man, though many of the citizens joked that he was half horse and half idiot. He was certainly known as a troublemaker and all-round inconvenience.

'Next time you two head off into the woods alone you might want to think about taking a guard with you. We wouldn't want you to get hurt now, would we, Princess?' He smiled, flashing his pearly white teeth.

'How kind of you, Isaac,' Ariadne responded bluntly, 'but we can look after ourselves, thank you. And besides, you are hardly a guard.'

Isaac's face dropped. 'Okay, okay, there's no need to be rude,' he said as he trotted after them. 'I was just trying to help. My father tells me the morning patrol found Reapers at the northern border yesterday.'

Isaac's companions nodded in agreement.

'Reapers? Really?' she replied sarcastically. 'That's the best you can come up with? Reapers haven't been seen near the city for hundreds of years. They wouldn't dare and if it were true, we'd know about it.'

'Ok Princess, whatever you say. I'm sure it was just a branch that attacked that deputy, Melbourne. Though it is quite a nasty cut he has on his arm now.'

Isaac looked smugly at the girls and trotted away, taking his band of make believers with him. Although Isaac's father was very well respected and was the captain of the royal guard, Ariadne doubted that Reapers had really come so close to the city. She shuddered.

'He always has something to say, doesn't he?' grumbled Ariadne.

'His stories are as wild as his hair,' replied Elda.

Ariadne laughed and shook her head as they continued walking towards the Palace.

They reached the Palace and stepped through the huge golden doors, their footsteps echoing along the marble arched corridors.

Her head thrown back playfully and eyes gleaming, Ariadne was beautiful. Even more so when she laughed, Elda thought as she walked alongside her. A loose headscarf encompassed the mountains of luscious black locks that tumbled off Ariadne's shoulders and down to her hips. She was dressed in a blue cotton shirt with golden embroidery and a pair of light, loose-fitting trousers, perfect for combat. Even in such attire and dripping with sweat, she looked beautiful, much to the dismay of her suitors' sweethearts.

Elda had never been jealous of Ariadne. Instead, she supported her and shared in the satisfaction of her triumphs. And besides, Elda had a likeable quality about her, not to mention a bagful of confidence and guts too. She was incredibly kind and would often cheer people up with her witty humour. This charm had resonated especially with Ariadne's twin brother, Amir, who was smitten with her. Though she had no time for relationships, as they were a luxury she couldn't afford, this didn't stop her from fantasising about Amir. He was tall and handsome. His caramel skin was soft to the touch and his eyes shone like beacons from his chiselled face. Elda tried to ignore these feelings as much as possible. She didn't want to be distracted, but he was so charming, and it was becoming increasingly more difficult to avoid him. She knew that nothing could ever happen between them. Royals and commoners weren't allowed to date. And anyway, she had her own dreams which didn't involve boys.

Elda wanted to become a Shaman, a type of powerful magician that had been around for thousands of years. The Shaman were an ancient Arcadian tribe that combined elemental and materialistic magic. More recently, they had become an elite society of powerful Magi. They taught magic to young scholars to the highest standards and were considered the fiercest Magicians in all the Arcadian realms. Some say that this was due to the people of Osaria being part Magi and part Grigori. To become a Shaman, you must be chosen as an apprentice by the high council and for this to happen, you must excel in your studies and be top of all your classes. Elda hoped one day to be chosen for this great honour.

The royal court was full of intelligent professors and academics from all over the world. They travelled many miles, across realms and seas, all to answer the call of Ariadne's father, King Cyrus. The King had commissioned them to educate his children in all areas, from mathematics and geography to combat and riding. This meant the best scholars and most qualified professors were teaching the students each day. The king's generosity spread to Elda and the other children at Court too, and they were allowed to attend lessons and learn from the masters. Elda excelled in her studies, but her attention wandered to Amir, who sat one desk in front of her.

Ariadne, however, struggled academically and often needed extra help, which Elda provided graciously. The students' lessons were varied and each day they completed training in many different areas, such as archery, orienteering and climbing. Their abilities were tested at the end of each year in a ceremony known as the Arcadian Trials. When a group completed their final trial successfully, they could be chosen as apprentices by professionals and academics. They could join the royal guard, become healers, train to be scholars or even become a Shaman. The trials were designed to test the knowledge of each student and to see how well they worked as a team by delegating and helping each other. The high council watched over the games too, and from the results chose potential apprentices to join their ranks. Elda was extremely excited about this aspect of the trials, wanting nothing more than to fulfil her dream of becoming a shaman.

The trial teams were organized by Professor Burmir, who had been their teacher since they were very young. Burmir knew each student well and tried to put everyone in a team that would value their unique skill set. He was a lovely, but odd man. Short and stout with a long grey beard and round framed glasses, he always seemed nervous and fiddled with his hands, but everyone was used to his odd jitters and gestures. He was always kind and nurtured every student to the best of his ability.

Ariadne and Elda were always placed on the same team. Their abilities complemented each other perfectly and their friendship made it easier for them to trust one another. The rest of their team members changed each time. This year's trial was more important than ever as it was the last one before they graduated. It was also special as it would be held in the mortal world. Every trial that they had completed previously had been held in Arcadia.

The Mountains of Bengal, the Forest of Hurst and the Kelasso Desert had been their previous trial locations, but this time it would be different. Visiting the mortal world was like a rite of passage for young Grigori and it was crucial that they put their best feet forward. Ariadne hoped they would get a few good swordsmen on their team and maybe a healer. A good team meant that they could complete their quest more easily.

The previous year they had been with the Pythos brothers, who were both strong and had their wits about them. They had come second, only beaten by Amir's team, who happened to stumble upon the last clue completely by accident. This year's task would be different. Rather than trials set by their professors, the new tasks would be real, unpredictable quests in an unknown land.

The new teams would be revealed the morning of the trials. They had one day to go, and everyone was excited.

CHAPTER 5

THE KING'S CHOICE

Ariadne walked towards the war room. The doors opened and Amir appeared, head hung low, his arms behind his back. He saw Ariadne approaching and straightened his posture, lifting his head back to its usual prideful position. He nodded at her with little expression and walked away. What was that about? Ariadne wondered as she proceeded through the doors.

The war room was made completely from marble, with tall ceilings and large windows. White columns lined the walls and the floor which had been painted with a huge map of the kingdom. It was used by Ariadne's father, King Cyrus, to plan military attacks as well as plotting Osaria's trade routes. The king stood at the far side of the room, pondering a small village near the northern border. He looked solemn, an uncommon expression for him. His long, grey hair was plaited down his back. He wore a deep purple robe, covered in golden, embroidered stars and small silver glasses perched on the end of his nose. As Ariadne approached, he looked up and smiled, the corners of his eyes crinkling with age.

'You called for me, Father?' she asked.

'Yes, my dear,' he looked down hesitating. 'We must discuss some very important matters and I'm afraid you will not like them.'

Ariadne frowned. She knew her father would not have called her here unless something important had happened. His glum expression made it even more obvious that he was about to break bad news. Perhaps this would explain Amir's odd behaviour.

'I'm sure you are aware of Osaria's history, my dear, but for clarity's sake I will refresh your memory. Centuries ago, when our ancestor, Eemos, led the Grigori to the eastern settlements, two Grigori tribes stayed behind. They refused Eemos' offer of sanctuary and rebuilt the valley of Arivale. The tribes were called Delos and Venator. Delos practised ice magic and Venator were skilled warriors.'

'Father,' Ariadne interrupted. 'What has this got to do with us?'

'Not many people know what has happened since we left Arivale, Ariadne,' he continued, ignoring her question. 'Very few people travel there and those who do rarely return. Delos were angry when they heard that we had befriended and bred with the Magi as equals. They believed that the Grigori were a superior race and that they should be in charge of all other species. Their king, Ezikeiel, demanded that we take control, forcing the magicians to serve us rather than live alongside us. Our leaders refused this offer, telling him that we would do no such thing. Ezikeiel threatened to attack with the combined armies of Delos and Venator. Knowing that many lives would be lost in this fight and unsure that they could win, Eemos struck a deal.'

'The Princesses!' Ariadne exclaimed as, with a growing sense of dread, she began to understand why she had been summoned.

For centuries, the future kings of Osaria had been married off to Arivalian royalty. It was common knowledge that this was done as a sign of respect between the two kingdoms, as they were the two most powerful nations in the whole of Arcadia. Darius' wife, Selena, was the latest of these brides.

'Indeed.' The King's tone was sombre as he took hold of Ariadne's hands. 'All of our future Kings are married to Arivale's royalty so that Delos can hold power in Osaria and profit from our kingdom's success. They take a proportion of our wealth and in return Delos stays away and we are allowed to live peacefully.'

'Peacefully! How are we living peacefully when we are being controlled? Why do our people not know about this?' said Ariadne as tears formed in the corners of her eyes.

She knew that the Delos Queens would have power, but never in a million years had she thought that they were anything more than respectful marriages. If what her father was saying was true, it meant that the Queens were nothing but pawns for Delos to control Osaria.

'That's just it, my dear. The people *are* free. They know nothing of Delos' power here and ignorance is bliss. What they don't know can't hurt them, but…' He paused. '… if the people found out about this there would be mass panic, and they would lose trust in us.'

'Maybe they should lose trust in us, Father,' said Ariadne. 'They've been lied to their whole lives, and you don't see a problem with that? If they knew then we could have risen up against Delos and taken back our control.'

'And risk the lives of all our citizens? No, child,' said King Cyrus calmly. 'Delos have let us live in peace for years. It would be unwise to disrupt that peace.'

'How can you break such horrible news to me without showing any emotion?' she responded angrily. 'Why are you not more upset about this?'

'My dear, as king I have had to make many hard decisions and as a father, I have had to make tougher ones. You are my youngest child and I have had this same discussion with each of your brothers. It pains me to see you like this, but just as your brothers have done, you will accept it and do your duty to the kingdom by safeguarding this secret...' He paused. 'Ariadne.' He spoke softly now. 'There may come a time when you must put the kingdom above yourself to protect our people. It is only at times like these that we really see what we're made of. You may think I'm weak for not fighting back, but perhaps I am wise for choosing a compromised peace over a deadly war.'

Ariadne didn't know what to say or do. This new truth was too much.

'I do not think you are weak, Father,' she admitted. 'I think you are strong for protecting our people.'

'Strength is a virtue, my dear. There will come a time when you too will need to be strong. A time when you must put the needs of the people above your own. A time when sacrifices must be made to protect this kingdom.' He looked into her eyes, admiring the strength he could already see in her.

Ariadne wasn't sure what he meant about sacrifice. She would gladly give up anything she had for her people, but the palace belonged to the king. The city belonged to the state and her family's wealth was not hers to give. She had beautiful clothes, gifts from suitors and more jewellery than she knew what to do with. She would give it all up in an instance if it meant protecting her kingdom but…

'I'm telling you this now,' her father continued, 'because your sixteenth birthday is approaching and…' He paused to gauge her reaction. 'You are almost of legal age to marry.'

The reality of Cyrus' words slowly sank in. She had always known that she would one day have to marry a stranger from some distant land, but she had always hoped that as she had so many brothers, they would be the ones to marry for obligation and that she could somehow marry for love. Either way, she hadn't expected to be married so soon. She thought she'd have years and years to choose a suitable husband. And besides, Darius and Selena were going to be the next king and queen. She was only fifth in line to the throne, so what did it matter who she married? Casper and Behnam were not married, and they were both in their twenties. She doubted that Amir would be forced to marry any time soon and knew that it had little to do with age and far more to do with her gender. This news had made Ariadne's dream of marrying for love almost impossible. She tried to clear her head. Her father was standing in front of her trying to read her expression. She thought for a moment. There was one thing that she still didn't understand.

'Why must it be so soon, father? Why can I not wait like my brothers and marry when I'm ready?'

King Cyrus looked down at the ground. 'My dear, you are a very special member of this family. You are the first daughter to be born in almost 200 years. That's seven generations of sons. It is said that women in our family carry a recessive Grigori gene, meaning that they are born with the same magic in their bones as pure blood Magicians. The men however carry a dominant Grigori gene, which allows less than an eighth of their Magi magic to be used. Delos has been marrying our kings to their princesses to stop Magi blood from entering the Osarian royal bloodline. Up until now, all of the women in our family have been full blood Grigori from Arivale. As part of the bargain struck by Eemos, he promised that all Osarian princesses would be married to Arivalians as a way to cleanse the bloodlines and keep an eye on any offspring that may have particularly strong magic.'

'Why would Eemos promise that!' cried Ariadne, tears now flowing freely down her flushed cheeks.

What a horrible way to keep Magi magic under control, thought Ariadne as she wiped her eyes. What's more, she didn't have any Magi magic. Okay, she had faint traces of Magi blood on her father's side and on her mother's side she was a normal mixture of Grigori and Magi, just like her brothers. She had no special powers like Elda and had never even considered trying to use magic. She was Grigori, and that was final. She knew that there were very few full blood Magi left in Arcadia. They had either been killed by Delos or had mixed their bloodlines with other Grigori clans. She understood how they could be seen as a threat to Delos, who hated anything that could be considered more powerful than their own magic. Even knowing this, Ariadne didn't agree with their logic. The Magi had been peaceful from the beginning. The only time they had ever fought anyone was when they were attacked first. She understood Eemos' negotiation of peace but hated that the wars of ancient men would play such a heavy role in her life.

King Cyrus could see the mixture of emotions in his daughter's face. 'I didn't make the rules, my dear.' He sighed. 'And I hate that it has to be this way.' He stepped forward holding out his arms to her and though she was full of resentment, she knew he was doing what he thought was best for the kingdom and welcomed his embrace. But why did it have to be her?

'It may help you to know that Eemos didn't make this promise lightly,' Cyrus told her. 'His own daughter was taken as a Delos bride and from that day he never quite forgave himself. He cast a spell on his bloodline that ensured only sons would be born. It worked for almost two hundred years, but you, my dear, were the exception. The magic did not account for twins.'

No, that didn't help, thought Ariadne who was almost out of tears, her skin red and blotchy and sleeve soaking wet. She couldn't bear to meet her father's eyes. Instead, she excused herself and turned towards the door.

King Cyrus reached out and grabbed her hand.

'We shall discuss this again later, dearest,' he said, the sadness in her eyes almost breaking his heart as she gazed up at him. 'Everything will be okay.'

CHAPTER 6

A ROYAL DISCUSSION

Family was very important to Ariadne, a trait no doubt instilled by her father Cyrus. Every evening, no matter what they had been doing during the day, they would all come together and eat dinner as a family. Ariadne always looked forward to her evening meal, and the company that it brought. Today, however, she was in a world of her own, lost in thought about the day's events. She hadn't yet had a chance to discuss her father's meeting with Elda, who was her most trusted confidant. As she walked into the dining hall, her brothers looked up and she tried to smile. The redness on her cheeks remained, but she hoped her crying would not be noticed as she took her seat at the table, opposite Amir.

Of Ariadne's brothers, Darius was her favourite. She knew she shouldn't have favourites, but it was hard when he was so great. Darius was her eldest sibling by quite a few years. He had just celebrated his 30th birthday and was trusted to work alongside his father as a privy council member, though he was more than just that. Darius was good at everything. Literacy, mathematics, politics, combat and riding were just a few of his talents. He was one of those enigmatic people that thrived on life. He was never boastful, nor prideful. He was a social butterfly and Ariadne couldn't think of a single person who disliked him. Even his competitors in sport and combat lost graciously to him. In her eyes, and in the eyes of many others, he was perfect, and she knew that one day he would be a perfect king.

Darius sat at the end of the table, opposite his father. They both wore formal tunics, Darius in blue and Cyrus in his signature purple. Sat beside Cyrus was his wife, Ariadne's mother, Helena. She too was equally as sociable as Darius. Helena and Cyrus had been childhood sweethearts. They had been in love since they were no older than Ariadne. Cyrus's first wife, Darius' mother, had been a Delos princess. She and Cyrus married out of obligation rather than love. When she passed away, Darius was only three years old. He needed a mother figure and Cyrus needed a queen. Helena was only too happy to accept Cyrus's proposal and gladly raised Darius as her own son.

A few years after they married, Casper was born. He was a babbling ball of noise from the moment he opened his eyes. He was headstrong and loud—in fact Helena had always said that anyone could hear him coming from a mile off. Casper had a wonderful sense of humour, albeit sometimes inappropriate. He was known for his pranks, a thing he was very proud of. He and his friends had once enchanted a firecracker to follow around a particularly serious council member, resulting in a huge commotion as well as a burnt bottom. Needless to say, Casper was disciplined for all his pranks, but each time Cyrus dished out his punishments, you could see a slight smile of humorous pride creep across his face.

Behnam came next, a strong and muscular prince, who always had young maidens vying for his attention. He had chiselled features and a strong jawline, and he was often told how handsome he was, which he knew all too well. Ariadne was often befriended by girls who wanted to date Behnam. They would ask her all kinds of questions about what he liked and disliked. It had happened so many times that now she had started feeding them false information. She would subtly sabotage them by telling them he loved what he hated and hated what he loved. Served them right for trying to use her like that.

Amir and Ariadne were the youngest. The twins were a great surprise to the king and queen and were considered lucky by many people. Amir had been born first, just before sunset on a warm summer night. Ariadne came a short time after, when the sun had completely gone from the sky. It was for this reason that they were often compared to Artemis and Apollo, the twin gods of the sun and moon. It always amused Ariadne that Amir was compared to the sun. He was so dull and serious. In many ways he was similar to Darius, but without the flare or enthusiasm to be social. He mostly kept himself to himself. Ariadne on the other hand was always off exploring with Elda. Even after ten years of adventuring around the palace, the grounds, the city and finally the woodlands, they would still find new and exciting places to explore.

The newest addition to the family was Darius' wife, Selena, who sat stiffly at the table next to him. Her skin was pale, and her hair was jet black. She was thin and bony, with a sharp chin and pointy nose. She never quite fitted in with the family, she was far too rigid and formal. She had been raised in Delos, not that she ever spoke about it. It was almost as if she were sworn to secrecy, or perhaps she just didn't care to share any personal details. She barely spoke unless spoken to, and hardly ever smiled. The only time Ariadne had ever seen her show any emotion was when she was shouting at servants. It seemed to infuriate her that things were done so differently in Osaria. She was nothing like Ariadne's family, who laughed almost the whole way through evening meals. Casper would tell stories about his pranks and Behnam would tell stories about his new loves. Darius and Cyrus would often speak of politics and diplomats, but they were never boring. The conversation was always kept light and humorous.

Cyrus beamed down the table at his family. He was at his happiest when surrounded by loved ones. On this occasion, his smile quickly faded, and his expression changed to a more serious one. He looked deep in thought.

'There is something that I need to discuss with you all,' he said, his voice soft but demanding. The laughter ceased and the mood in the room changed as they sat waiting to hear what their father had to say.

'As you may have already heard, we have faced a new threat, a threat that has been dormant for almost two hundred years. There was a Reaper attack on the northern border not three days ago and another two attacks yesterday morning.'

The expression on everyone's face was the same. Wide eyed and jaws open. They were shocked, even Ariadne who had heard it first from the irritating centaur, Isaac. She had assumed that he was making it up, but perhaps he really was trying to be helpful.

'This isn't an isolated incident,' Cyrus said glumly, reaching for Helena's hand. 'Reaper attacks have been reported by travellers from all around Arcadia. We heard not long ago that some of the villages on the outskirts of Kelasso had been raided. Kelasso are our allies so naturally we sent forces to help them. Little more than half our troops returned.

'Casper, Behnam,' he said softly, 'I will need you to aid the guard in protecting the outer villages.' They both nodded solemnly. 'If the Reapers continue their attacks, I don't know how long we can hold them back.' Cyrus hung his head.

This changed everything. Ariadne now understood why her father had been so insistent on her marrying into Delos. Delos were wealthy beyond words. They had three armies at their disposal and commanded power over everyone in the north. If the Reapers were back, then Osaria would need allies. Marrying into Delos could be used as a bargaining chip to secure forces to fight the Reapers. Delos wouldn't allow Osaria to fall, it was the main trading point in the east and funded much of Delos' army. But she knew a marriage would sweeten the deal.

Scared beyond relief, Ariadne knew she would have to leave her home, her family and Elda. Her sixteenth birthday was only a few weeks away and she knew that once she was old enough, her father would have no choice but to start her marriage negotiations. She looked at Darius, who had clearly already known about all this. He sat quietly, staring at his food.

Cyrus continued, 'We are gathering our allies as fast as we can, but it will take time, and there may still not be enough of us. Reapers don't travel far on their own, so there must be a swarm nearby which is bad news for everyone.'

A tear ran down Ariadne's cheek. She knew what had to be done.

'I'll do it,' she said softly under her breath.

'Hmm?' murmured Cyrus as he looked up.

'I'll do it,' she said, louder and with more conviction. 'I'll marry into Delos if it means keeping Osaria safe.'

An eruption of objections came from her brothers, but Ariadne had made up her mind. As much as she didn't want to go, it was her duty to protect the kingdom.

Cyrus smiled softly, proud of her decision and yet concerned for her safety. 'Let's hope it doesn't come to that,' he said wistfully. 'We still have time.'

CHAPTER 7

THE SECRETS OF THE PALACE

That night, Ariadne barely slept. Her room was too warm, and she couldn't get comfortable. Her mind wandered and her thoughts kept her awake. She tossed and turned until the early hours of the morning. Unable to bear it any longer, she got dressed, grabbed her hunting gear and satchel from her dresser and headed for the door. She carefully opened it, checking for guards as she crept out. The corridors were bare, solid marble and Ariadne's footsteps patted gently against it as she snuck through. As she reached the throne room, she spotted a small flickering shadow dancing against the far wall. Cautiously, she approached, staying hidden behind a large column. Ariadne could hear hushed voices whispering aggressively. She poked her head around the column to see who it was.

It seemed suspicious that anyone would be up this early. She wondered if she had stumbled upon a secret rendezvous or perhaps a lovers' quarrel.

Instead, she saw the angry face of Selena.

Selena was as cruel as she was beautiful and had never been fond of Ariadne. As a child all Ariadne wanted was Darius's attention. He would always spend time with her, and this made Selena jealous. Selena would often tease Ariadne and try to embarrass her at any opportunity. Now, Selena was arguing with a man in a dark hooded cape. Ariadne couldn't see his face, but his deep voice sounded rough, and he had a distinct accent. She couldn't place where this accent was from. It was raspy and cold, like nothing she'd ever heard before. She listened intently to hear what they were saying.

'It's time!' Selena's shrill voice insisted. 'We should act now.'

'We are moving as fast we can,' came the deep raspy reply. 'They won't attack without a promise of payment.'

'Listen carefully!' Selena growled. 'I am the future queen of Osaria, and you will listen to me.

If we do not act before the twenty-first, they will be too strong. I will arrange payment when I am queen.'

The twenty-first? That was Amir and Ariadne's birthday. Ariadne wondered what Selena meant about 'acting fast,' and what did it have to do with their birthday? She could hear footsteps in the distance and slipped further behind the marble columns. She heard Selena and the hooded figure slip away through the back room and head towards a spiral staircase that led down towards the courtyard below.

The footsteps grew louder as two guards walked past chatting quietly, oblivious to the secret meeting or Ariadne's presence behind the marble column. Ariadne knew Selena would not be pleased if she discovered that she was being followed. As soon as the guards disappeared, she slid noiselessly from her hiding place and took off after them.

On reaching the top of the staircase Ariadne looked down and watched as Selena followed the man out into the courtyard. A huge black horse was pawing impatiently at the sandy floor as he waited for his master. With one hand on the bridle, the man stepped into the stirrup and swung himself up onto the back of the horse.

He reached down as Selena handed him a scroll on which Ariadne could see the distinctive seal of the Royal crest shining in the fading moonlight.

After a final exchange of words, Selena stepped back as the man pulled on the reins and spun his horse round, ready to leave. As he dug his heel in and the horse reared up, Ariadne spotted a shiny object fall from a pocket in his cape and bury itself in the sand. This went unnoticed by Selena, who turned as the horse galloped off and headed back into the Palace.

Ariadne waited to be sure the coast was clear. Why was Selena meeting with the stranger? she wondered. What did she mean about 'payments' and 'attacks'? Was Selena sending troops to fight the reapers? Somehow Ariadne doubted it. Unable to stem her curiosity any longer, she ran down the spiral stairs into the courtyard. Kneeling down, she buried her fingers into the sand, curled them round the object and pulled it free.

Confused, she frowned down at what appeared to be a large gold coin, about the size of her palm. Glinting in what was left of the moonlight, she examined the engraved symbol on its face,

a flame pierced by an arrow. It wasn't an Osarian symbol,

she was sure. In fact, she had never seen anything like it before. It certainly looked important and was clearly very valuable so how had the rider been so careless?

As the moonlight faded and the horizon brightened, Ariadne put the coin into her satchel and looked up at the sky. The sun was peeking out from behind the palm trees, with the Trials almost upon them. She had planned to go hunting that morning. She always hunted when she wanted to clear her head. There was something about the natural silence and calming scenery that made her feel at peace, but with all that she had seen and heard rushing through her mind, she knew this had to be dealt with first.

She didn't want to disturb her father as he thought Selena was lovely and wouldn't believe a word of it. No, she had to talk to someone who would trust her words and judgement. Someone who knew Selena was capable of wrongdoing, and most importantly, someone who could do something about it.

Casper and Behnam had already set off on their trip and Amir would be of no help so the only person she could go to was Darius.

Hoping he was awake, she approached his chamber and knocked quietly on the door. No response. It was still early, so she didn't expect him to be up, but she knew he sometimes had trouble sleeping and read to keep himself occupied. She knocked again, this time a little louder.

'Come in,' came the reply.

Darius was sitting up in bed, reading as Ariadne had guessed. He was surprised to have a visitor so early in the morning and looked out of the window to gauge the time. It must have been about five. He took off his reading glasses and placed them on the bedside table.

Shutting the door behind her, Ariadne perched on the end of his bed.

'What are you doing, Ari?' he asked.

'I need to talk to you,' she replied.

'About Delos? It was very brave of you to volunteer as you did,' he smiled.

'No, not about that,' she frowned.

'Oh?' he responded, looking confused.

'It's about Selena, I think she's up to something.'

'Ariadne…'

'I know it sounds crazy,' she stopped him in his tracks, 'but I heard her talking to a hooded man just a few minutes ago and they were saying something about an attack and how they had to act quickly…'

'Ariadne, stop,' he repeated and pointed towards a window seat on the far side of the bedroom where Ariadne could see the faint silhouette of Selena, fast asleep, with a book in her hand.'

'But that's impossible,' she exclaimed. 'I saw her, I swear I saw her!'

'You must have seen someone that looks like her,' he replied. 'She fell asleep there last night and hasn't moved. I've hardly slept, and I would have noticed if she'd left. You know I'm a light sleeper.'

Ariadne couldn't believe it. She knew that she had seen Selena. There was no doubt in her mind.

'That can't be right, I know what I saw!' she said again.

'I want to believe you Ari, but Selena hasn't done anything wrong, she's been asleep.'

At this moment Selena yawned, opened her eyes as if from a deep slumber.

Sitting up she put her book on the floor and stretched her arms upwards.

'What's going on?'' she asked innocently.

'Ariadne thought that she saw you in the throne room talking to someone about attacks of some kind. But I've already told her that you've been here all night.'

Selena looked surprised and shook her head, 'Oh, really? No, it wasn't me. Maybe it was someone else, or maybe you just imagined it?'

'I didn't imagine it!' Ariadne insisted. 'I saw you, Selena.'

'Now, now, dear,' Selena sang in her most patronising voice. 'I know you don't like me, but that doesn't mean you can go around making up vicious rumours about me. You really must think more carefully about what you say about people. You may end up hurting someone…' She paused. '… or perhaps yourself.'

Ariadne was so frustrated she let out a cry.

Selena had made her look like a liar and what was worse, Darius believed her. She glared at Selena. She opened her mouth, about to speak, when Darius cut her off.

'I think you've said enough, Ariadne. You should leave now.' He said firmly as he got out of his bed and walked her to the door.

'But!'

'No buts, go back to bed and get some sleep. You'll feel better in the morning,' he said as he opened the door and waited for her to leave.

Ariadne walked past him, then looked back to see Selena smiling behind Darius' back.

'Argh!' she groaned as she stormed away.

Despite him telling her to leave, Ariadne couldn't believe that Darius was ignoring her warning. He knew full well that Selena was capable of something like this, and yet she had somehow convinced him that she had been with him all night long.

Ariadne made her way back to her room. She knew she wouldn't be able to sleep, so instead, she wandered through the gardens before heading back up the stairs towards her chambers. The guards looked puzzled as she strode past, but they were never much good at keeping her inside so didn't take that much notice of her being out at such an early hour.

When she reached her room, Ariadne gathered her things and packed what she thought she might need for the trials. It was almost time to go, and her mind was full of one hundred other things, but at least, she thought as she headed for the door, she'd be with Elda.

CHAPTER 8

THE TRIALS

Ariadne walked to the edge of the forest. Professor Burmir was giving each of the competitors the name of their team and a place on the starting line.

Ariadne was part of Team Kiba, named after the ancient Grigorian tribe. She was glad to be paired with Elda, though her other teammates came as an unwelcome surprise. Amir, who was rarely on her team for anything, had been forced upon them. Ariadne was sure this was a mistake. They were so different, and their skills weren't exactly complementary. Amir thought he was right about everything, and Ariadne had no patience with him.

They were both trained in sword combat, which Amir excelled in, but Ariadne preferred to use her bow. Ariadne was excellent at geography and cartography, the study of maps, but was otherwise untalented at academics. Amir on the other hand was good at math and literacy
and considered himself a future scholar. They argued about everything and nothing, a classic sibling bond, so when Amir joined them at the starting line, Ariadne wasn't the only one in shock. It was clear that he hadn't expected Ariadne to be on his team either.

Approaching with caution, Amir waited for her inevitable rant about how unfair it was, but to his surprise none came. Ariadne was far too upset to rant and remained unusually quiet for several minutes. Amir thought this must have been a record and although he was also annoyed at the team pairings, he kept it to himself. One thing he was glad of though, was Elda's company.

Amir and Elda had an interesting friendship. Often, they would only see one another whilst Ariadne was around. There were a few occasions, however, when they had been free of her, some classes that they took that she did not.

It was in these moments that their friendship really blossomed. They had a lot in common and enjoyed each other's company, but sometimes Elda gave him mixed signals, which left him confused. She would ignore him when they were around Ariadne and act like they were the greatest of friends when they were alone. He wasn't sure what this meant, but perhaps spending this time with her during the Trials would make things clearer.

The final member of the team, to Ariadne's dismay, was Isaac, just about the most useless team member Ariadne could think of. He had no common sense, was always messing around and had average fighting skills at best. Isaac's father was a highly decorated member of the Royal Guard. He was strong and brave and must have had quite the shock when Isaac was presented to him as a baby. A bundle of curls and gurgles, with no idea how the world worked, not that he was any better now.

To be fair, Ariadne felt sorry for Isaac. His mother had died in childbirth and his father was a very busy man. This meant Isaac had been left to run wild around the city. With little input from his father and no mother to raise him; it was hardly surprising that he was a mess. She imagined this was why he was so hyper all the time, always vying for attention and yet dreadful at timekeeping, which was probably why he hadn't shown up for the team introduction. A great start thought Ariadne. With the games due to start in a few hours they had little time to plan, and despite Isaac's absence, they had no choice but to start without him.

At the edge of the forest, Elda and Ariadne perched on a small boulder and began formulating a plan as Amir busied himself taking inventory of their equipment. A good excuse, he thought, to stay out of Ariadne's way. Each team had been offered a selection of weapons from the armoury. At this point it was hard to choose what equipment they might need, as they didn't know where they'd be going or exactly what they'd be doing. Amir had selected four daggers, which he thought were a safe bet. He'd also picked up their food rations for the three days they would be away and a compass from the Professor's table.

In turn, Professor Burmir had carefully handed Amir four shimmering orbs, telling him to be careful not to break them.

He'd reminded Amir that the portals in the orbs were their only way of getting back to Arcadia from the mortal world. As to where in the mortal world they would end up, they had no clue. In addition to the daggers, he'd chosen a long sword for himself, but had left the others to choose their own weapons. He thought Elda would want a sword and Ariadne would probably want a bow, but he didn't want to face

their wrath if he got it wrong.

With no sign of Isaac all morning, Ariadne was becoming more and more frustrated. She hadn't slept and her head was pounding with everything she'd witnessed earlier. Trying to calm herself down, she thought about what kind of place they might visit on their trial. The Trials would usually only take one day but for this final assessment three days were allocated. Ariadne really hoped it was somewhere tropical, but she knew the mortal world wasn't known for its weather so didn't hold out much hope.

With the trials due to start at eight o'clock sharp and only ten minutes to spare, Isaac galloped over the hill,

his hooves pounding on the ground, a large saddle

bag in tow, overflowing with who knew what.

'You're late!' Ariadne shouted as he approached.

'Sorry, I overslept!' He yawned.

Ariadne rolled her eyes. 'Typical,' she snapped as the trial horn blew loudly, summoning the teams to return to Professor Burmir at the edge of the forest. With no time to waste, they set off for the rendezvous, leaving Isaac clueless as to their plans.

Waiting with Professor Burmir was the tall figure of Melbourne, Captain of the Royal Guard and one of the kingdom's most fierce warriors. He'd been asked to referee the trials and, like Isaac, was a centaur. Not that this would give their team any advantages. Melbourne was strict but always fair. He would monitor every move they made through an eye portal and make sure they were on track.

Eye portals were an ancient form of magic, used to keep watch over those too far away to visit. Many kingdoms used them to communicate as they were much faster than sending a letter. The portal was cast into a small cylindrical disc, which was attached to a pair of glasses. It only covered one eye,

as there had been issues in the past with people walking into walls or falling down stairs when not paying attention to their surroundings.

This always amused Ariadne as she remembered that Casper had once fallen off his balcony whilst wearing a pair.

Kiba and the other teams stood on their marks at the forest's edge, ready for the start of the race. The first part of the trial was always the same, a sprint to the campfire in the centre of the woods. Here they would find a selection of portals, each offering a glance at what the task might be. Amir handed everyone their orbs, fixing his own to his signet ring. They were given one orb each, though each contained a portal that could transport many people. It was just a security measure in case someone got lost and needed to return home. Isaac secured his orb to the hilt of his sword and Ariadne did the same with her dagger. Elda wore a silver necklace to which she attached her orb, tucking it into her shirt for safekeeping.

Melbourne blew his horn, and they were off. Amir and Ariadne charged ahead, using their Grigori speed to reach the clearing as fast as they could. If they got there first, they would have first pick of the quests and hopefully take the lead.

Elda followed closely, riding on Isaac's back, his hooves hammering the ground as they galloped toward the camp.

Amir and Ariadne arrived first at the clearing, panting. It was a large, wooded space with a lit fire pit in the centre. Positioned around the dancing flames were six glowing portals. As they approached, images flashed before their eyes. They were previews, a fractured series of pictures, hinting at what each trial would entail. Amir was intrigued by a purple portal on the far side of the fire pit. It showed flashes of a battlefield and a great victory. To the right Ariadne focused on an Arabian desert scene, full of dancing figures and dangerous snakes.

The contestants had to be careful and choose wisely, as each portal would take them to a completely different place. They needed to agree as a team and choose a task that they could all excel at. They had to act quickly, so as not to be left with the worst one. More and more teams arrived at the campfire to view the orbs. Once a whole team had arrived, they could place their hands on the orb and start their quest. As Isaac galloped into the clearing, Elda slid off his back and rushed to Ariadne's side.

'What do you think? Elda asked excitedly. 'What are the options?'

Amir joined them and said, 'There's a village trapped on a snowy mountain that needs help and another with a castle under siege.'

'And here,' Ariadne chimed in, 'there's a sorcerer who's controlling a mortal kingdom and a temple under attack by raiders.'

To their left a team had already decided on their quest and placed their hands together above the orb and vanished, taking it with them. At the far side of the camp another team took their pick, disappearing with a flash.

'Come on, we need to choose,' said Elda as she walked round to a different orb. 'What about this? It looks like a pirate ship?'

Another team vanished.

'Come on! We need to pick one!' barked Ariadne.

'This one seems fine,' said Elda as another team vanished.

'Okay,' said Ariadne. 'All in agreement?'

They looked at each other, eyes darting around and nodding.

'Let's do it,' said Amir trying to sound sure of himself.

Placing their hands over the shimmering portal, Ariadne took a final deep breath and with Isaac's hand last to touch its glowing light, they vanished.

CHAPTER 9

A NEW WORLD

Her vision blurred, her eyes stung, she felt the heat around her melt away and in its place warm tingling water gushed. Still submerged, Ariadne opened her aching eyes. All around her light beams pierced the water, shimmering softly. She looked at her feet and saw silvery sand all around. Pushing off from the seabed, she surfaced from the water. She turned, looking for the others as Elda and Amir emerged looking as shocked and confused as she was. The water in front of them began to bubble and Isaac appeared sputtering and coughing. He seemed more dramatic than usual, thrashing around in a panic. Ariadne looked around for land and to her surprise saw an island teeming with fishing boats and bustling people.

Isaac continued to splash, which was odd as she knew that he could swim. He would eventually wear himself out if he continued and a drowned teammate was not the start they were looking for.

'Ahoy there!' came a voice from behind.

They turned to see a small fishing boat sailing towards them. 'You look like you could use a ride to shore,' shouted a kind-looking fisherman.

Before they could answer, Isaac clambered to the side of the boat and pulled himself up.

'No! exclaimed Amir thinking the weight of an almost fully grown centaur would crush the small boat. But to everyone's surprise Isaac was no longer the centaur they knew. They stared at him in amazement as he lay on the deck gasping for air, trying to catch his breath.

Slowly they gathered at the edge of the boat and peered down.

'Isaac,' said Elda cautiously. 'I don't want you to panic even more, but have you seen your legs…?'

Isaac turned pale as he looked down. 'I'm...I'm human,' he stammered as he reached out to touch his legs. He turned to Ariadne and drew back her hair from the side of her face. 'And so are you.'

Ariadne touched her ears, which had turned from delicate and pointed to fat human ears. Amir checked to find that his elven ears were also gone. Elda too felt different, like she had lost part of herself. Confused, they all climbed aboard the boat, thankful that the fisherman had offered it to them.

'I'm Joe,' said the fisherman as he shook Amir's outstretched hand. 'Is your friend, ok? He seems a bit shaken up.'

'He's fine, said Ariadne. 'He's just a bit panicked, that's all.'

'Well, I should think so too,' laughed Joe. 'What's he doing out here if he can't swim, eh?'

They didn't know how to reply to this without sounding completely mad. They couldn't very well tell a mortal that they had used a magic portal which had transported them to the middle of the sea, now could they?

'What is this place?' asked Amir, pointing to the shore as he tried to change the subject.

People were rushing around, going about their business in quite a hurry. Maybe they were too far offshore to tell, but it looked to Amir as if they were running from something.

'Oh, this old place is called Torcello,' the old man smiled. 'I've lived here my whole life, and this isn't the first time I've had to fish people out of the water,' he laughed.

'Well, we're very grateful to you, Joe,' responded Ariadne.

'None quite like you though,' he said, then frowned as he looked down and noticed Ariadne's golden dagger, covered in elven inscriptions. 'You might want to hide that girly. Some people here aren't too fond of your kind.'

Ariadne was shocked. She didn't think humans knew anything about Arcadia. Perhaps a few had heard stories, but Arcadians were forbidden from revealing themselves to mortals. She did as she was told and hid her dagger under her cloak as the shore grew closer and the lower town became clearer. It was obvious that the residents were in distress. Many held bags and cases, overflowing with belongings and others dragged children into houses, slamming the doors shut behind them.

'What's wrong with them?' asked Elda, the concern in her voice evident.

'It's harrowing season,' Joe answered. 'It shouldn't be starting for another day or so, but it looks like they got here early.'

'Who got here early?' asked a very pale Isaac who was clearly not yet over his escapade in the water.

Ariadne wasn't sure if this was due to the distress of the people or the fact that he'd lost two of his legs.

'The pirates, lad. You really aren't from around here, are you?'

As the boat sailed into the docks and pulled alongside a small mooring, Joe whispered, 'Best we stay here for now and keep quiet,' as he pulled out some old sheets from the back of the vessel and threw them over the boat, covering them all.

Crouching down, Ariadne peeked out from under the sheets onto the now empty street in front of them as the first sounds of the pirates' angry shouting and loud clattering echoed down the streets.

'What's happening? whispered Amir. 'Why are there pirates here?'

'Quiet, lad,' hushed Joe.

The cobbled street was littered with empty baskets and abandoned market stalls. The doors and windows of every building were shut tight and locked. Footsteps approached from the far side of the docks and two figures came into view.

They were young, no more than sixteen and covered in dirt.

The smaller of the two was a red-headed girl dressed in an oversized white shirt and dark baggy trousers. There was a boy with her, about a foot taller and dressed similarly. Silver swords hung by their sides. They were arguing over a large linen sack brimming over with all sorts of trinkets.

'Are they the pirates?' whispered Elda, looking underwhelmed.

'Aren't they too young? questioned Ariadne.

'That's how they get 'em,' said Joe shaking his head in disgust. 'They take the little 'uns and train 'em to be just as bad as the big 'uns.'

Isaac tried to stand up to get a better view. 'We could rescue them,' he said, wobbling as he struggled to balance on his new legs.

'Careful!' said Amir as he grabbed Isaac's arm, trying to stop him falling over. But it was too late. Isaac stepped backwards, lost his footing, tripped and toppled over the side into the water. A loud splash followed, making everyone wince.

'What was that?' they heard the pirate boy ask as he walked over to the water's edge. 'I heard a noise.'

Isaac reached up and grabbed the side of the boat and kept as quiet as possible.

He was shielded from view by the wooden moorings in front of him, but the ripples from his fall were rolling towards the dock. The others ducked further below the large sheet, hiding themselves amongst the fishing nets and barrels.

'Who's there?' the boy shouted and drew his sword as he approached the boat. 'I know you're there!' Bending down, he reached for the sheet, only a second away from revealing the group's hiding place, as Isaac pushed himself away from the boat, grabbed the side of the mooring and began thrashing around in the water.

The pirate stood up and took his hand away from the boat.

'You there!' he shouted. 'Show yourself.'

Isaac paddled awkwardly to the side of the dock, still finding it difficult to swim. Thankfully his bulky arm muscles hadn't been affected by his transformation and he was able to pull himself up and out of the water and sat on the edge of the dock, his flimsy legs still partly submerged in the water below.

The pirate boy looked down at him, probably trying to assess whether he was a threat. Isaac was somewhat offended when the boy turned his back, in order to talk to his companion.

If he was in his usual centaur form, he would have had no trouble dealing with this tiny pirate.

In human form however, and unable to walk properly without falling over, Isaac decided it was best to let this one slide.

The two pirates were now bickering over what to do with Isaac. Before they could decide, and hoping to catch them off guard, Amir and Elda jumped from the boat and landed, weapons drawn. Elda tried to use her magic, but she couldn't seem to summon it. Behind her, Ariadne stood on the dock, her bow poised and ready to jump into action. Their sudden presence startled the pirates, who drew their own swords in retaliation. The redhead girl could barely hold the sword upright and was clearly struggling with its weight, but the boy looked like he knew what he was doing as he stood ready to defend himself.

'We outnumber you two to one,' said Elda, hoping this logic would discourage a fight. 'Surrender and no one will get hurt.'

'Never!' the girl shouted, but as she went to charge at them the boy grabbed her by the collar and lowered his sword.

'Drop your swords,' commanded Amir.

Reluctantly they did, kicking them towards the edge of the dock and raised their hands in surrender.

'Now that's what I'm talking about!' said Isaac excitedly. 'Take that, pirates, you don't want to mess with team Kiba!'

Their triumph turned to concern as they realised that instead of looking scared or apprehensive, the pirates looked smug, grinning at each other. The boy wet his lips and whistled tunefully. Almost immediately footsteps could be heard coming from the surrounding alleyways as the boy made direct eye contact with Elda, a glare she found both threatening and intimidating at the same time. Then, from each alley came hordes of pirates, all bearing weapons and looking menacing. Now it was their turn to be surrounded.

'I think you'll find that now we outnumber you,' smiled the boy, showing off his pearly white teeth. 'Drop your swords, surrender and no one will get hurt,' he said mimicking Amir's words.

'Harumph!' grunted Elda in frustration as they dropped their weapons.

The girl stepped forward and gathered them together as the boy picked up his own sword, pointed it at Elda and gave her a wink.

Amidst the hoard of pirates, Ariadne watched as a woman covered in scars appeared.

She wore a red bandana and strode forward, her

demeanour powerful.

She clearly had control of the men around her.

'Well done, Danny,' she said, gesturing to the boy as he lowered his sword. 'And you Keira. Maybe you're not useless after all.' She laughed. 'Okay lads,' she called out. 'You know what to do,' and the pirates closed in.

CHAPTER 10

IN FIGHTING SHAPE

Danny bit into his apple. He was leaning against the railing of the upper deck, looking down at his new captives. They had been tied together and left at the base of the stairs, surrounded by crates and barrels. Their hands were bound behind their backs, but their eyes were not covered. He felt guilty that after his own kidnapping, he had helped with someone else´s, but in his defence these captives had surrounded him first and the pirates could have done a lot worse than kidnap them. He wondered if they had been locals from Torcello, or whether, like him, they had been visiting.

They didn't look like small town folk. In fact, he'd never seen anyone who looked quite like them. They were dressed like warriors, in leather armour with enough weapons to rival even the ship's armoury, but they were children, about the same age as Danny. Keira had helped herself to a shiny gold dagger, confiscated from the captives, which she had snuck past Melanie's guards. Apart from that, their belongings had been dumped in a pile at the side of the ship. Danny had noticed that many of their weapons were decorated with strange engravings and inscriptions. He tried to read them, but he couldn't understand the language.

The two boys were tied back-to-back, Isaac, he had heard the fairer one being called. He had been an odd sight, with muscles bulging out of his sleeveless leather vest, but incredibly thin legs, which he was unable to stand upright or balance upon. His hair was dark brown and frizzy, he looked like he had been struck by lightning a few hundred times. He sat with his legs stretched out in front of him, moving them up and down as if they were new. The other boy looked more sensible, with similar clothing to Isaac, but a much more regal demeanour. He had his legs crossed and a solemn look on his face. He assumed this was perhaps due to their recent abduction.

Danny turned his attention to the girl who had originally confronted them. He had learnt that her name was Elda, from the other girl, who had been very loudly shouting during their kidnapping. Elda was staring at him with harsh eyes. Danny wished

that she had been given a hood or had her eyes bound, anything to stop the intimidating looks.

It wasn't his fault that they had been taken. When he had whistled for Melanie and the others, he thought that they would just take their weapons, or maybe scare them off the island. He didn't know that they would be captured. A foolish mistake, he thought. What did the pirates want with them anyway? They already had a large enough crew, and it was unlikely that this group of nomads would be any help to the pirates. Danny realised that this was exactly what he had done. He was now as much a pirate as any of the crew. At first, he had resented Isabelle and the Captain for taking him against his will, but he actually quite liked being a pirate. After the first few weeks he found his sea legs and made the most of his time, learning as much as he could about maps and navigation as well as battle training. He had also been spending time with Isabelle, which of course he was thrilled about.

A few days after his own kidnapping, Isabelle had come to him, completely unprovoked, and asked him to take a walk with her.

Lost in conversation, they'd walked the length of the ship what felt like a hundred times. Her mysterious demeanour melted away as he learnt

more about her. She apologised for taking him against his will, saying that she had no choice. She explained that if she didn't take new hostages to train as crew members, then the captain would have been very angry with her.

'I had to take someone, and you just seemed like the right fit,' she had told him. 'And you do seem to be enjoying yourself.'

Admittedly, Danny was enjoying his time on board the Hellbourne Princess. It was far more interesting than working at the fish stand in Highshore. He liked the excitement of not knowing where they would be going next, not knowing who they'd meet or what they'd find. Most of all he enjoyed Isabelle's company. She told him about her childhood and life before the pirates. She had lived with her sister in Renée and had worked with the circus. She told him about the places they'd visited and the people they met,

travelling constantly and never settling down. Danny liked hearing about her life. It made him feel closer to her. He was still unsure if she liked him the way that he liked her, but at this point, he didn't care. It was just nice to be with her.

After that day their walks became a habit. Every evening after lights out, they'd sneak onto the deck and talk for hours. It was these conversations that kept Danny going, and why he always looked forward to nightfall. He was thinking about Isabelle that morning, standing on deck, watching the captives. He didn't mean to stare at them, but in all honesty, he had zoned out, daydreaming about being with Isabelle once more. He was truly smitten.

A roar of cheering interrupted his thoughts. The armoury had been unlocked and the crew were eager to train. The training duels had become Danny's second favourite part of the day. He got to watch outstanding displays of skill and force as well as try his hand at defeating others in combat. He was surprisingly good for his age and size. His father had taught him well when he was younger, though he had not practiced since his father left. He was catching up quickly, managing to beat men twice his size.

In fact, his size had become an advantage when fighting, as he could easily duck and move out of the way. He was agile and quick, much to his competitors' dismay. It had become a sort of challenge for Danny to beat each of the crew members in combat.

He was not good enough yet, but with practice he hoped to be. Today's training was especially important to Danny, as Isabelle was attending, and he wanted to impress her. He knew it was foolish, as he doubted that he had any chance with her, but there was no harm in trying. He had long since forgiven her for the whole kidnapping thing as he knew that if it wasn't for her, he'd still be working the fish stand with Oliver. She had seen something in him, chosen him to join the crew, and now he wanted to prove to her that he was worthy of the job. Today, the pressure was on. The captives were pushed aside, and the deck was cleared. Danny headed down the stairs to join the crowd. Melanie ordered the training swords to be brought out. These swords were blunt but still lethal if used correctly. Training wasn't used to harm one another, just to prove that they were a better fighter. The swords were presented in the middle of the deck and the first challengers were chosen.

A large, bald man named Enoch, with arms the size of tree trunks stepped forward. Opposite him, Khan, a man with long braided hair entered the ring. They took up their weapons, ready to duel. Khan was thin but fairly muscular, Danny had seen the damage done by his sword and bet Khan would win this duel.

'Begin!' roared Melanie, as the two men charged at each other.

Khan made the first move, swinging his sword at Enoch, who stepped back, narrowly missing its metallic edge. Enoch grunted as he swiped back at Khan's outstretched arm. Khan ducked and rolled, ending up behind Enoch who turned to meet his sword. The metallic clang reverberated around the deck as the swords came together. Enoch pushed his sword down, edging it towards Khan's face. In a battle of strength, Enoch would be the clear champion, but sword fighting was about more than just strength. Khan spun around and dropped to the floor, extending his leg and sweeping Enoch's feet from under him. He sprang up quickly and pointed his sword at Enoch's exposed neck as he lay on his back, defeated.

'We have a winner!' exclaimed Melanie as she entered the ring and held Khan's hand high up in the air.

The pirates roared, excited to see who the next competitors would be. Mouse was selected to fight against Nico, one of the newer recruits. Nico was tiny compared to Mouse, who towered over him like a mountain. After removing Meg from his top pocket and placing her on top of a nearby barrel, Mouse stepped into the ring. This fight was significantly shorter.

With one blow of Mouse's sword, Nico was sent flying across the deck. The crowd laughed. Melanie announced Mouse the winner as Nico stood up, rubbing the back of his head. More fights followed, seeing a fearsome pirate

named Isla beaten by her older sister Beatrix and Seb Dyer, the ship's punching bag, almost cut in two by the sword of his sparring partner, Enzo.

Danny was enjoying the show, seeing if he could guess the winner of each battle before the end while Isabelle stood at the top of the stairs, watching the fun from an arm's length. Keira, too, was watching eagerly. She had climbed up the mast to the crow's nest and was watching from above. Danny knew it wasn't his job, but he felt responsible for Keira. As irritating as she was, he knew that she too had been taken from her home and, though she did well at hiding it, she'd been as scared as him.

The first night on board the ship, all the new recruits had slept in the large bunk room below the deck. The room was full of hammocks that swung softly with the waves.

Danny had heard Keira sobbing softly from her perch high up against the ceiling beams.

In some ways Danny and Keira had a lot in common. They both grew up in Highshore and had very little money. They had both resorted to stealing food at some point in their lives. The only difference was that when Danny's father left, he arranged for Danny to work at the fish stand with Oliver. This meant he could afford food and

lodgings. He wasn't paid much, but it was enough to get by. There were also the anonymous cheques that he had received. He had often wondered who his mysterious benefactor was, deep down he hoped that it was his father, showing that in some way he was still looking out for Danny. Logically it made sense. Who else would send Danny money?

Keira, on the other hand, had lost her mother very young and was left to fend for herself. She had first been admitted to an orphanage. Danny saw her hanging around there once or twice, but after a few weeks there, she ran away. Danny didn't know why, and he didn't ask. That was the last time he saw her until last month in the market. He assumed that she had been living on the streets, but he couldn't be sure. He watched her in her tower, playing with her stolen dagger. Perhaps being kidnapped was the best thing for her.

It meant that she would be fed and clothed and in a strange way be part of a family. But Danny didn't presume to know her mind. Out of nowhere he heard a crash and saw barrels rolling towards him. He stopped one with his foot. Everyone turned to see what the fuss had been about. The captives, who it seemed everyone had forgotten about, were on their feet and arguing with Enoch.

'Get it off her!' shouted Elda. She stood between Enoch and her friends. Her hands were still bound but she looked fierce and poised to attack. Enoch, in his defeated state, had kicked over a group of barrels, one of which had landed on Ariadne. Elda tried to move it herself but her bound hands made it difficult. She pushed her weight onto the barrel and managed to move it slightly, leaving enough room for Ariadne to roll out from under it.

'What's going on?' barked Melanie, clearly furious the games had been interrupted.

No one said a word. Melanie's threatening tone and even more threatening appearance intimidated them all into silence. The captives, however, stood their ground as she approached.

'You,' she said, looking at Elda. 'Tell me why I shouldn't throw you and your friends overboard for disturbing our fun.'

Elda didn't know how to respond. She hadn't done anything wrong and yet Melanie was blaming them for Enoch's rage. Before she could come up with an answer, Melanie turned to the crew.

'How should they be punished?' she yelled with a cruel smirk upon her face. 'Should they walk the plank?' The pirates cheered. 'Or...' She thought for a moment. 'Should we make them fight to stay aboard?' The pirates cheered again. 'Who will fight the captives?' she called out. 'Who will teach these prisoners a lesson?' Almost half the crew volunteered. 'Hmmm,' pondered Melanie as she looked from one crew member to another until focusing on Danny, who stood quietly at the back. She'd noticed he'd been watching intently, but had failed to volunteer so proclaimed, 'It's only fitting that the person who brought us these captives should have the pleasure of fighting them,' she said with a wicked smile.

Danny slowly realised what she meant and had no time to reject her proposal. Not that it would have done him any good if he had tried. The crew turned to look at him, cheering as he awkwardly made his way to the front. He already felt bad about having them taken in the first place, and now he had to fight one of them as well. As he approached the centre of the deck, he looked up to where

Isabelle had been standing. He had hoped that her presence would make him feel better, but she was nowhere to be seen.

He stood next to Melanie, trying not to look too concerned. He had never fought in front of a crowd so large, and he didn't know what the crew would do to him if he lost.

'And which of you will fight our champion?' asked Melanie.

Danny stared at the captives, but he didn't fancy his chances. They stood shoulder to shoulder in their leather armour, fists clenched, and eyes narrowed. Each of them looked like they could do some damage. He had sized them all up when they had been captured and he had been watching them all morning. If it were up to Danny, he would've chosen to fight Ariadne. Elda seemed much too threatening and certainly had a grudge against Danny. Isaac could barely walk, which would make it an unfair fight. Amir was much larger than Danny and had a defensive quality around the others. Ariadne, on the other hand, was a similar size to Danny and though she looked like a very capable fighter, she looked slightly less threatening than Elda. She would still be a worthy opponent, Danny thought. Unfortunately for Danny, he didn't get to choose. And even worse, Elda raised her hand.

CHAPTER 11

MERCY

The fight began like any other. Strike after strike, met by a defensive blade. They danced around the deck, stepping back and forth as the crowd cheered them on. Danny could tell from the start that Elda was a great fighter. She handled her weapon with ease, like she had been practising her whole life, but there was something strange about her technique. She attacked with precision, setting up what should have been her final blow, but when she got to this point, she seemed to retreat. It seemed as though she was waiting for something to happen, but what could she have been waiting for? Perhaps she was just sizing him up waiting to see what he would do next? After all, Danny was holding his own, something Elda probably hadn't expected.

Elda was in fact frustrated. She had been training for this kind of thing for as long as she could remember, and yet her magic didn't seem to be working. She knew that she couldn't be too obvious with her magic, mortals would not respond well to it, so she was trying to cast small spells. Elda had tried a tripping jinx, which had failed miserably. She then tried to subtly push him backwards with the force of a wind spell. Nothing was working and she couldn't figure out why. She felt completely unprepared. She knew how to fight with a sword, but she had never had to rely on it to defeat her enemies. Her usual tactics included portaling and vanishing, which confused her opponents and allowed her the element of surprise as she suddenly reappeared with a dagger to their throats. Of course, now that she was in the human realm, these were not viable options… or so she thought.

Leaping back over a coil of tattered ropes, Elda found herself up against the side of the ship. Danny moved towards her, brandishing his sword. Catching her off guard, as she tried to focus all her energy on summoning her magic, Danny managed to thrust his sword towards Elda's throat.

He hesitated, unsure of what to do next.

Elda could see the merciful look in his eyes, he didn't really want to hurt her. She used this momentary lapse in his confidence to lunge to the side, escaping Danny's outstretched sword. He snapped out of it, jumping back into battle. Instinctively, Elda tried again to draw on her magic. She focused on the coils of rope at her feet, willing them to entangle Danny's ankles. She felt the usual energy rush through her body and into the tips of her fingers, but to her dismay, nothing happened as Danny's sword engaged hers once more. Neck and neck, using all her might to hold her ground, Elda focused on the rope, this time slowing her breathing and concentrating every ounce of energy on the coils.

At last! The ropes began to squirm and like a writhing serpent rose up and wrapped around Danny's feet. Looking down in shock as the coils tightened, Danny tried to kick out as Elda shoved him, sending him flying backwards and landing on the deck with a loud thump.

As the cheers from the pirates stopped abruptly, Elda couldn't help but grin. She pointed her sword down at Danny, who lay confused on the floor.

'I guess this makes us even?' He looked up smiling nervously.

Elda looked at him and lowered her sword. 'You spared me once,' she said, 'and I will show you the same mercy, but... we are not even.'

Danny quickly freed his ankle and stood up as Melanie pushed through the crowd and grabbed him by the ear.

'Ow ow ow!' he exclaimed. 'You're hurting me!'

'I'll do more than hurt you, lad,' said Melanie as she marched him off like a scolded child. Danny could hear the laughter of the pirates echoing around the deck behind him.

Elda turned and rejoined her friends, both exhausted and relieved that her magic was still at her disposal. She shared a smirk with Ariadne as Amir put his arm around her and gave her a welcoming hug. Not that the moment of relief lasted long as Isaac stepped forward and, facing his friends, raised an important question, 'So what happens now?'

Dragged up the stairs with Melanie keeping a tight grip on the top of his ear, Danny dread to think what his punishment would be after embarrassing the crew like that. Personally, he didn't see anything wrong with being beaten by Elda. She had won fair and square and was clearly a great fighter, although he couldn't quite work out how he got his feet so tangled up in the rope. Unfortunately, he doubted that Melanie had seen it that way and what was worse, they were heading straight for the captain's quarters.

Since joining the crew a month ago, Danny had only seen the captain a handful of times. He rarely left his quarters or bothered to address the crew. Isabelle, too, was hardly ever seen in daylight. She and the Captain spent their time locked away plotting who knows what. And whatever it was, Isabelle never spoke of it during their nightly walks on the deck.

To all intents and purposes, Melanie was in charge of the whole ship, so Danny must have been in big trouble if they were going to disturb the captain. There were many rumours on board about what Isabelle and the Captain did all day. Some of the crew claimed that they were working on finding the location of buried treasure and others said that they were trying to find a good place to bury their own riches. None of these rumours could be proven, as they were very secretive about their work and no one, not even Melanie, was allowed into the captain's private chambers.

As they approached the door, Danny overheard fierce whispers. 'It's now or never,' one voice said.

It sounded like the voices were arguing, but they were so quiet that Danny couldn't make out any more words. Melanie cleared her throat loudly and the whispers stopped as she knocked heavily on the door three times.

'Enter,' came the captain's response, a voice that sent shivers down Danny's spine.

Danny took a deep breath and tried to compose himself as Melanie let go of his aching ear and pushed him through the door.

The huge figure of Captain Moreno was sitting behind a large oak desk, his clenched fists resting on a map spread out before him. Isabelle leant over the desk beside him, studying the map as Danny shuffled in.

Although he kept it to himself, not unlike the rest of the crew, Danny was terrified of the captain whose reputation of harsh brutality went before him. The fierce glare that met him as the captain raised his head did nothing to make him feel any less afraid.

Lowering his eyes so as not to antagonise the Captain, Danny glanced down at the map and cocked his head to one side as Isabelle whisked it off the desk. Rolling it up, she placed the map into a leather tube and slid it onto a shelf atop a nearby cabinet before returning to her position at the captain's side.

'What have you brought me?' asked the captain, his displeasure at being interrupted evident in his tone.

'I plan to throw him overboard,' growled Melanie, looking at the captain for approval.

'No!' exclaimed Isabelle.

Despite the seriousness of his situation, Danny was pleasantly surprised at this interruption. Isabelle had been discreet in showing any signs of fondness towards him. Perhaps there was more to it? Maybe she did feel something towards him?

The captain looked quizzically at Isabelle before responding, 'And why would we want to do that?'

'He was defeated in combat by one of the strangers we took aboard.'

The Captain and Isabelle again looked at each other, a momentary glance that seemed to share a thousand words.

Danny hoped that they would pat him on the shoulder and say, 'Never mind, lad, better luck next time,' but somehow, he thought this was unlikely.

'Well?' questioned Melanie, clearly hoping for his approval, as she knew the crew enjoyed it when someone walked the plank.

'Lock him in the brig,' said the captain.

'But...' Melanie began to reply until the look on the captain's face stopped her in her tracks.

Danny felt almost bad for her, apart from the fact that she had wanted to kill him. She seemed genuinely upset as once again he was marched away.

On reaching the door, he turned and stole a quick glance back into the cabin and saw the look of relief on Isabelle's face as Melanie yanked him through the opening by the scruff of his neck.

Frog-marched down into the bowels of the ship, they reached the brig, a box-like structure of metal bars with a damp wooden floor that stank of stale sweat and other unpleasant odours.

'Have fun with your new friends,' sneered Melanie as a huge black rat scuttled across the floor and she pushed Danny through the door, 'and don't think you'll be so lucky next time.'

Turning to look back at her as she slammed the door shut behind him, Melanie didn't know whether to be surprised or even more angry at the look on Danny's face as he sat down on a wooden bench.

He knew he was supposed to be upset, but all Danny could think about was the look of relief on Isabelle's face. He smiled softly to himself. However long he had to spend in the brig now was eased by this pleasant thought.

Danny looked around. Peering through the darkness, he could just about make out the outlines of other prisoners when a familiar voice spoke up.

'Hello again.'

It was the girl he'd fought, her voice calm as it floated from the shadows. She sat against the wall of the neighbouring cell, her head tilted backwards, eyes focused on Danny. The other girl sat next to her, with a glum expression on her face. Behind them Danny could see the two boys, against the wall in the far cell.

'Great,' muttered Danny under his breath. First, he'd been forced to fight an angry stranger, whose kidnapping he had accidentally brought about and now, he was locked in a very small, confined space with her and her friends. This day couldn't get any better, he thought.

'Look,' said Danny. 'This has all been a huge misunderstanding.' He tried his best to sound confident, but his words faltered. He wanted to tell them all how sorry he was and that he too had been kidnapped, but settled for, 'Let's start over, shall we?' he asked hopefully.

The girl looked at him, eyes narrowed. She was suspicious of his truce offer. After all, he had tried to kill her only a half hour ago. She remained silent, as did her companions.

'I'm Danny,' he continued. "What are your names?'

Before they could answer, the door was flung open. Everyone turned, waiting to see which of the rough-looking guards had come to check up on them. To their surprise, it wasn't a guard. Isabelle entered looking nervously around the room for Danny. When she saw him, she sighed with relief and made her way over to him, kneeling at his side.

Danny stepped forward, meeting Isabelle at the bars of his cell. Isabelle's eyes were red and puffy, as if she'd been crying.

'Isabelle,' he said. 'What are you doing here? What's wrong?'

'I'm sorry,' she replied, reaching out to hold his hand. 'I tried to have you released,' she looked at the floor, 'but when I asked, the captain got angry. I don't think he likes our friendship.'

'Our friendship?'

'He knows everything. He knows that we see each other at night and...' She paused. '... and how I feel about you.'

'How...how do you feel about me?'

Isabelle seemed to ignore his question but held on tightly to his hand as Danny tried to pull it away.

'It's complicated,' she said, staring into his eyes. 'I don't want to be the reason he hurts you, but I've really gone and put my foot in it now.'

'What do you mean?'

'He was angry that I asked for you to be released, so as punishment... he's going to let Melanie have her way and throw you overboard.

'Why would he be angry about that?' asked Danny. It didn't seem to make sense to him, especially if he already knew about them meeting each night.

'I got on his bad side and trust me; you don't want to be on his bad side. He is a cruel man, Danny, remember that.' She brushed a tear from her cheek.

Danny looked at her intently. 'Why are you with him if he's cruel to you? Why don't you just leave?'

'I can't!' she snapped.

'Why not? If you're not happy…'

'I'm bound to him, Danny. He owns me and unless you have a few thousand gold coins spare then there's nothing you can do. If I ran away, he'd only find me again and I'd be punished. You have to believe me, I want nothing more than to leave, but it's not worth it…' She paused and looked round as if looking for anyone spying on her. 'Look, none of that matters now, I'm here to help.' She forced a smile but had tears in her eyes. 'They're planning to throw you all overboard tomorrow morning at first light, so you need to escape tonight.'

From her cell next door, Elda's ears perked up. She hadn't meant to eavesdrop on the conversation. Well okay, she had, but in her defence the room was small, and Isabelle's voice wasn't exactly quiet. She'd only vaguely followed the conversation, until she heard what was in store for her and her friends.

'They're going to throw us all overboard?' asked Elda. She wanted to make sure she'd heard correctly.

Isabelle's eyes darted over to Elda's cell. 'Yes,' she spoke clearly, immediately looking back towards Danny.

Elda raised her eyebrows as Isabelle continued her conversation, showing no interest in the other captives. How rude, she thought. If their fate was tied to Danny's, then it was their right to know and at least be part of the conversation. As a feeling of dread crept across her mind Elda suddenly realised that Danny could be the one, they were meant to help in their quest. They had wasted the first day of their trial being kidnapped by him and now they were stuck in the same cell as him, waiting to be killed. 'Great start!' she muttered to herself, but then, what if all this was meant to happen? Maybe the point of their trial was to get into this mess and then help Danny escape?

Logically, this made sense. Team Kiba could help Danny escape from the pirate ship. Maybe get him somewhere safe and then their trial would be over. Danny was obviously a decent fighter, but he had no chance of escaping the ship alone.

There would definitely be guards, and how would he get out of the cell, let alone off the ship? Swim? He would have to commandeer a boat, which Elda doubted he could row by himself. Elda turned to the others, in a whispered voice explaining that Danny could be the key to their trial.

'Are you sure?' asked Ariadne. 'He doesn't look too bothered to me.'

'Look,' said Elda sternly. 'He got us kidnapped. He was picked to fight me. He gets thrown in the cells with us. He's about to get thrown overboard. In fact, we're all about to get thrown overboard. That can't be a coincidence. He must be important to the trial in some way. And regardless of our personal distaste, if we don't escape with him…'

'I agree with Elda,' Isaac jumped in quickly. It was obvious that the thought of going for another swim was not on Isaac's to do list.

'As do I,' said Amir, nodding furiously.

'Ok then,' said Ariadne. 'What's the plan?'

'Shh!' hushed Elda. 'Let's try and hear what they've got planned.'

Isabelle leant closer to the bars of the cell. 'Danny, you need to get off this ship and go somewhere where he won't find you,' she said earnestly.

Danny thought for a moment. 'Come with me, Isabelle! We can go anywhere and start over. He'll never find us.'

'It doesn't work like that. He has spies all over the world. He'd find me wherever I go. The only way that I could ever be free is to pay him what he's owed,' she said, wiping away another tear with the back of her hand.

Danny knew he wasn't going to leave Isabelle at the mercy of the captain's cruelty and, not fancying his chances of keeping her safely hidden from the captain if they ran, he decided the only way forward was to somehow, buy her freedom.

'The map in his study...' said Danny, 'what does it lead to?'

'It's a treasure map he's been studying for almost ten years. It supposedly leads to the wealth of Xander, a legendary pirate of great renown. But Danny, it's impossible to decipher.'

'What other choice do I have? I won't leave you here with him!'

'Oh, Danny, you don't have to do this.'

'Of course, I do, I...,' he faltered for a moment, then said with confidence, 'Isabelle, you chose me to join the crew because you saw something in me, and I want to prove that you made the right choice.'

'Thank you,' said Isabelle, smiling softly as she touched his cheek. 'If you really want to do this, we'll have to act quickly. The map is hidden above the liquor cabinet in the captain's study. If I cause a distraction to draw him out, you can sneak in and grab it. But promise me you'll be careful.'

'I will,' promised Danny.

'I'll cause a diversion at midnight. Wait until you hear the watchmen's bell. When you get the map, head to the starboard side of the ship, that's where the rowing boats are kept. You can use one for your escape.'

'After I find this treasure,' said Danny, more optimistically than he felt, 'how do I find you again?'

'In two days', time, we'll be docking at Port Gracious, to restock the ship. You'll be able to find us there.'

'Okay, Port Gracious, it is,' said Danny. 'But one last question. How do I get out of these cells?'

'Leave that to me,' she said, grinning. 'I have just the person and she owes me a favour anyway.'

She'll need to, thought Danny as Isabelle, with a final squeeze of his hand, turned and disappeared off into the darkness.

CHAPTER 12

THE GREAT ESCAPE

Isaac leant against the bars of his cell and whispered, 'Now that sounds like my kind of quest!'

It was now clear to everyone what needed to be done. Their mission was to help Danny find the treasure and free Isabelle. They were all relieved to have some kind of idea of their end goal, but they still needed to convince Danny to let them help him. Amir doubted that he would just let them join his escape plan. They had all been hostile towards him and hadn't exactly gotten off on the right foot. Amir was also still cautious of helping Danny and didn't trust him at all, but he knew the last thing their quest needed was an impromptu drowning.

Ariadne turned to Elda. She, too, seemed doubtful that Danny would trust them enough to let them help. What would they do if he refused?

'How do we convince him?' she whispered to the group.

Danny was now pacing his cell, much too preoccupied to notice their conversation. Regardless, they kept their voices hushed.

'We could just ask him,' shrugged Isaac. 'He did sound sorry about kidnapping us, and if he was really a bad person he wouldn't have bothered to apologise.'

'That's true,' agreed Elda. It was certainly the simplest way to go about it. Her own plan would have been a mixture of threatening then convincing him, but Isaac's plan was surprisingly sensible.

'So, are we agreed?' asked Isaac, looking around for reassuring expressions.

Elda and Ariadne nodded while Amir offered no reassurance.

Taking this as a 'Yes,' Isaac cleared his throat loudly.

Danny glanced up. Met by four pairs of eyes, he looked like a deer who'd just heard a twig snap in the woods.

'What?' he asked, turning to see if someone new had entered the brig. With no sign of anyone, he turned back to the group, more than a little confused as to why they were staring at him.

'We want to come with you,' said Ariadne confidently.

'Not a chance,' responded Danny, shaking his head.

'You're not to be trusted.'

'We could help you get the map you were talking about. And you'll need help rowing the boat,' Ariadne persisted.

Danny thought about this. He knew she was right. There was no way he could lift the boat over the edge of the ship by himself, let alone row it safely ashore. On top of that, he had no idea where he was going and didn't even own a compass. It also occurred to him that all four of the other captives were dressed in armour, and he knew that at least Elda could fight. Indeed, when he ran into them, they'd been travelling through Torcello alone and seemed to know what they were doing. They were clearly his best hope if he was to find the treasure and free Isabelle.

That said, he didn't want them to know that he needed their help. He wanted to seem confident and in control so… 'Okay,' he said, placing his hands on his hips and with his voice raised slightly, but not so much as to alert any guards. 'You may come with me, on one condition.'

'And what is that?' asked Ariadne, amused by his air of what she could see was false bravado.

'You must help me free Isabelle,' he said, then, as his arms dropped down to his sides, 'Okay look, I, I don't know if I can do it alone,' he admitted, 'but please, if you come, you must help me free Isabelle.'

Ariadne turned back to the group. This was exactly what they needed. Danny had asked for their help, meaning they didn't have to lift a finger in convincing him. Ariadne smiled at Elda, before meeting Danny's eyes once more. "We're in".

As midnight approached, Ariadne hugged her arms. The cells were freezing and the dark green trial jumpsuit she wore was sleeveless and made of thin material. The Arcadian crest was embroidered into the front of the suit in gold stitching. Everyone participating in the trails wore one of these jumpsuits and Ariadne never understood why. They were supposed to be blending in, not sticking out like a sore thumb. Luckily, they were also given brown, leather armour, which was old and worn and hid the crest quite well. She doubted that the flimsy armour would make any difference to her, if a sword or dagger were thrust in her direction, and yet in the freezing cell, she was grateful for another layer. The outfit would have been perfect for the homely, desert climate that she was used to, but this was nothing like home. The ocean was cold, especially at night. Even in the midday sun, the sea exposed them to winds from each corner of the earth. Ariadne shivered as Elda shuffled over and wrapped her arm around her shoulders. She was grateful for Elda's warmth. Her mind wandered. They sat silently as the time ticked by slowly. She was no further in figuring out what Selena was up to and wondered if she should tell Amir. Ariadne had already mentioned it to Elda, whose advice was always helpful. Elda had told her not to tell Amir quite yet. There was the potential that he wouldn't believe her, which would just cause an unnecessary argument. As well as this, it was almost midnight and with the plan almost afoot it would be foolish to divert anyone's attention with another problem to solve.

When the midnight bell rang out, signalling the guards to swap lookout posts, everyone got to their feet. The bell was immediately followed by a rustling sound and soon after this, the door swung open. To Danny's surprise, Keira stood in the doorway, five foot nothing and yet still managing to command the room. She held a large bronze key in her grubby hand. Why was Keira helping with their escape? Danny had no time to ask. She headed over to his cell, unlocking it and quickly moving on to the next one. Once she had freed all five of them, she led them from the brig and out into the corridor without a word.

When they reached the door to the top deck, Keira stopped, checking to see if the coast was clear. She turned to the group.

'I'll get you into the captain's study,' she told Danny. 'Everyone else, head to the far side of the ship where Isabelle has a boat waiting for you.'

Danny had no idea when Keira and Isabelle had become such good friends, but in that moment, he didn't stop to question it and followed Keira towards the Captain's quarters. Carefully keeping in the shadows, everyone else headed for the escape boat, grabbing their belongings that had been carelessly left on deck.

The heavy oak door of the captain's quarters was guarded by two men. Danny recognised Khan from the fights earlier but didn't know the other man. As they approached quietly along the deck, the door opened and they jumped back, hiding in the shadow of a sturdy support beam at the base of the staircase that led down onto the deck.

Isabelle and the Captain walked arm in arm as she led him towards the far side of the ship, then, pointing up at the night sky she said whimsically, 'Isn't it a beautiful night?'

'Yes. Indeed, it is,' responded the captain, following her gaze.

Spotting Danny and Keira out of the corner of her eye as they reached the bottom of the stairs, Isabelle made sure to keep the captain's attention on the stars as she looked back and beckoned the guards to follow her. They looked at each other, confused, but did as they were told.

Danny couldn't help but notice how comfortable Isabelle was giving commands. Not that it mattered, as the most important thing now was the coast was clear. They quickly darted out from the shadows, leapt silently up the staircase and through the now unguarded door to the captain's quarters.

Closing it behind them with a sigh of relief, Danny looked around. He hadn't noticed on his previous visit how big the room was. The first half featured a large wooden table, full of books, maps, and scraps of paper. Bookshelves lined the walls until they met an arched doorway. Through the arch, Danny could see a large double bed, fitted with purple, satin sheets and covered with plump pillows. Above the bed, a huge stained-glass window allowed moonlight to stream in and send colours dancing across the sheets. Danny quickly walked to the cabinet where he had seen Isabelle hide the map. Reaching to the top, his hands brushed against cobwebs and layers of dust, before finally clasping onto the leather tube. He pulled it down to examine. He was sure that this was the right one. The same faded brown colour, the same tattered leather strap and the same strange, jagged symbol on the crest. Just to be sure, he opened the lid, checking to see if the map was still there. It was safely intact. He pulled the strap over his head and shoulders, securing the tube on his back then turned to see Keira snooping through the captain's things. She had a habit of taking things that weren't hers, but Danny chose to ignore this. She had, after all, just helped him steal the map and had also managed to take the cell key from right under Enoch's nose. Her unique skill set had come in useful after all.

They left the room quietly, making sure that no one saw them leave, and made their way down the stairs and across the deck towards the getaway boat. Elda saw them coming and began quietly moving the boat towards the edge. As they arrived, Danny climbed into the boat where the others were waiting.

Reaching down for Keira, he held out his hand. 'Come on,' he said. 'It's time to go.'

'I'm not coming with you,' she said, stepping back. 'I told Isabelle I'd help you, but I have no reason to leave the ship.'

'We have to go,' urged Elda as she swung the boat over the side of the ship.

'As you wish,' said Danny. He felt strange and a little sad to leave Keira on her own. But then again, she did seem to really like the pirate life, and she fitted in wonderfully. 'Thank you for your help, Keira. I'll never forget you,' he told her with a smile.

'Until we meet again, then.' She saluted him with a cheeky grin and scuttled off into the darkness.

Elda climbed aboard and with Amir's help began lowering the boat into the waves. Hitting the water with a gentle splash, Isaac and Danny pushed away from the ship with ease then grabbed a pair of oars each and within minutes the ship had disappeared into the night as they headed out into the unknown.

CHAPTER 13

TROUBLED WATERS

A thick sea fog engulfed the boat when Elda woke. She was nestled under Amir´s arm and, realising she'd dribbled slightly in her sleep, quickly wiped her mouth before anyone could see.

'Why didn't you wake me?' she said angrily as she sat up and looked round at the choppy water. It must have been early morning. The sun was rising, and beams of light were piercing the fog but there was no sign of land as far as the eye could see. 'Anybody got any idea where we are?'

'Ask him,' responded Ariadne, nodding her head towards Danny, who was perched at the front of the boat, studying the map. 'He's been staring at it since the crack of dawn.'

'Danny!' called Elda. 'Can we see the map?'

He turned around, breaking his concentration. 'Urrm… yes, ok,' he said as he swung his legs round to face the group and placed the map in the centre of the boat.

Everyone gathered round, taking in the maps tattered features. It was old, but not ancient. Perhaps ten or fifteen years old? The parchment was worn, probably from constant handling and the salty sea air. The map showed the five mortal kingdoms surrounded by oceans. It was bordered by tiny gold lettering in a language that Danny couldn't understand. At first, he had thought they were just decorative, but he guessed from the slanted curves and delicate placement that it meant something more. Small golden stars decorated various spaces around the map, but there didn't seem to be any pattern that he could see.

In the top hand corner of the map, was a small wax seal, the same seal as was shown on the side of the leather tube. Elda studied the map with great interest and although she had never seen it before, thought it looked very familiar. The image was of a burning arrow, one which Ariadne recognized immediately. She reached into her satchel, pulled out a large gold coin and showed it to the group. The same image featured on the map was pressed into the coin.

'Where did you get that?' asked Amir.

Ariadne passed the coin to Elda. 'Selena's henchman,' she replied in a worried tone. She decided it was time to let everyone know of the strange events surrounding Selena's rendezvous with the horseman.

She explained that she had never trusted Selena, nor did she like her for that matter. Admittedly, Ariadne did get a bit carried away as she described the numerous things that she disliked about her dear sister-in-law.

No one was more confused than Danny as he examined the coin. 'I've seen this before,' he muttered, stroking his thumb across the coin's embossed surface.

'Really?' asked Ariadne, who was keen to connect the dots. 'Where?'

Danny looked up at her, a confused expression on his face. 'Hang on a minute,' he said as he tried to process Ariadne's words. 'Do you think your sister-in-law is after the treasure too?'

'No, that wouldn't make sense,' replied Ariadne as she cleared her mind and began to think. 'She doesn't need money. She's married to the future king.'

'Ariadne!' snapped Amir, annoyed at her for revealing too much.

'Did you say... future king?' asked Danny looking shocked.

Everyone remained quiet as Ariadne looked at Elda, who looked right back at her with a *well go on then, what are you going to say now*, look on her face.

'Oh dear,' grimaced Ariadne as Amir shook his head, clearly annoyed. 'Well... urm, yes,' she smiled at Danny, flashing her pearly white teeth. She knew that if she offered no explanation then a whole host of questions would follow. Technically, there wasn't any rule against mentioning her Royal status, she thought, trying to cover her slip up. 'Our father is King and our eldest brother, Darius, is next in line to the throne. Selena is his wife. Now, where did you say you'd seen the symbol?'

Too excited to think of anything other than her Royal blood, he ignored her question, responding instead with, 'So you *are* Royalty!' he exclaimed, giddy with excitement.

Ariadne smiled. She was glad of Danny's excitement. She had never had to explain her status to anyone. At home, everyone knew who she was and kept her at arm's length because of it. Not many people felt comfortable being themselves around her, as they were intimidated by her father. Most people treated her as an extension of him. She liked that Danny seemed excited about it even though he knew nothing of her kingdom… or did he?

'The symbol?' she asked for the third time.

'That same symbol is printed on anonymous cheques I receive each month.'

'That's strange,' said Ariadne, unable to imagine how the two things were linked.

'Can we please focus on the map?' sighed Amir as he tried, unsuccessfully, to draw attention away from the symbol which he heavily suspected *was* Arcadian.

Danny was bursting with questions but saw Amir's frustrated expression and decided to leave his inquiries for another time. He was right, of course. They needed to concentrate on the map and free Isabelle.

Isaac picked up the tube, holding it up to his eye like a telescope. To his surprise a tiny square of paper slid down from inside and hit him in the eye. 'Ow!' he winced and dropped the tube as the paper fell to the floor. Picking it up as he rubbed his eye, Isaac could see it was covered in bits of sticky leather. 'Maybe this will help,' he said as unfolded the paper and held it up to the light.

On the page, a faint handwritten message could be seen. The paper was creased and yellowed with the edge having been clearly ripped from the spine of a book.

'What is it?' asked Elda.

'It looks like a letter,' said Isaac as he began to read…

Day 113

The mortal world is harder to navigate than I had first thought. The days are getting shorter and colder. We travelled through a small fishing village near Renée today. It was calm and peaceful, and I wondered if this was the sort of place, I'd one day settle. We have moved a lot over the last few months, never staying in the same place for more than a few days. I have thrown the Reapers off our trail. I lost them just outside of Murano. We are almost out of Orbs, so will have to find a more permanent home soon. Adanion is safe for now. He sleeps through most nights and cries very little. He has your eyes, my love. He misses you, as do I.

Forever yours

Xander

Elda took the letter from Isaac. She re-read it, noting a few things that stood out.

'Xander,' she said softly. She didn't know of anyone with that name, but she did recognise the name Adanion. Adanion was a famous Grigori name, given to the very first king of Delos. But that was centuries ago, and this letter had been written far more recently. Was Adanion code for something else? Or was it a coincidence? Either way, they had to find out if Delos had anything to do with it. What could a mortal treasure hunt have to do with the Grigori? Did this mean that Xander was Arcadian?

'He mentions Reapers,' said Elda looking at Ariadne, the look of concern evident on her face.

'And Orbs,' added Ariadne. 'It's obviously connected to Arcadia.'

'Whoever this Xander was, he wasn't human,' blurted Isaac without thinking.

Danny laughed. 'What do you mean "he wasn't human" what else could he be?'

The vein on Amir's forehead was bulging. It looked as if it were about to burst. 'Isaac!' he growled.

'Only joking,' said Isaac nervously. *Gods,* he thought, knowing Amir wouldn't let him forget this one.

Elda glanced at the others. They had almost forgotten that Danny knew nothing of their world and was completely out of the loop.

'We should tell him,' whispered Ariadne.

'Don't you dare!' threatened Amir under his breath. 'It's forbidden and might affect the trial.'

'Amir's right,' Elda whispered to Ariadne. 'We could get in serious trouble.'

'I'm not deaf!' said Danny bluntly. He could see their expressions were serious and guessed he was missing something important. 'Can someone please explain what's going on?'

Ariadne didn't care about the consequences. She had to know what the symbol meant and how it was connected to her kingdom. If Danny knew something, she wanted to know what it was. She thought about the best way to tell Danny that he was in the presence of two Grigorian elves, a magician and a centaur, but before she could break the news softly, Isaac opened his big mouth.

'Well...'

'*I* have to tell him, 'Stated Ariadne. 'If we do get in trouble, I'd rather the blame be on me.'

'No!' shouted Amir, but as he lunged across to cover her mouth, the boat wobbled.

'Stop it!' yelled Ariadne as she tried to kick him away and pull his hands from her mouth. They struggled and scrapped as only siblings could, forcing the boat to rock widely back and forth.

Elda didn't know what to do. She wanted to pull Amir off of Ariadne, but that would allow her to spill Arcadian secrets. Before she could decide either way, Isaac did it again…

'None of us are human!' he shouted over the commotion.

Danny stared at them as if they were mad.

'We don't look like it now,' said Isaac, his manner strangely calm, 'but Ari and Amir are elves, I'm a centaur and Elda can shoot magic from her palms. Oh, and we live in a realm called Arcadia.' Isaac obviously didn't think that the introduction of a new world and multiple new species was a big deal for Danny.

'That's not exactly right,' corrected Ariadne. 'We're Grigori and Elda's part of the Magi.'

Amir and Elda said nothing. Instead, they both stared at Danny, waiting to gauge his reaction.

Sat at the front of the boat, Danny looked completely stunned. He didn't know how to process such mind shattering information. How could any of it be true? There was no way.

'I know it's a lot to get your head round, Danny,' said Ariadne as she put her hand on his, 'but right now we have to figure out what this has to do with Delos and if they're involved, it can't be good.'

'You're an elf and…' he looked at Elda, 'she's a wizard?' He shook his head. 'None of this makes sense. How do you expect me to believe any of this!'

Elda sighed. Now that Isaac and Ariadne had revealed their biggest secret, she had no choice but to help with damage control. 'I'm not a wizard,' she said sharply, clearly offended by this suggestion. 'I'm a magician, and as for you believing us, you don't have much of a choice. You'll never figure out this map alone.' She pointed to the golden inscriptions. 'It's written in ancient elvish. You need us.'

'And we need you too, Danny,' added Isaac as Elda shot him a stern look. This wasn't a good time to tell Danny about the Trials. He was already overwhelmed, and she didn't want his tiny human brain to implode.

'Oh, for gods' sake, just show him,' said Ariadne. 'You managed to move the rope, maybe your magic is getting stronger?'

Elda thought for a moment. She was curious to see if her magic had returned and there was no harm in trying, who knows it may come in handy. Holding her palm out in front of her, Elda concentrated her energy on creating a flame and after a few short seconds felt the tingling sensation in her fingertips build up, until a small spark flew from her hand. With that obstacle overcome, she closed her eyes, slowed her breathing. As she opened her eyes, her hand exploded into a flame of light which left Isaac grinning and Danny with a look of horror and fascination on his face.

'Believe us now?' asked Elda as, with a smile, she clenched her fist and the flame subsided.

CHAPTER 14

XANDER'S MADNESS

As the late afternoon sun began to sink in the sky, Amir spotted something on the horizon. The waves had calmed, and the fog had cleared, but the mood onboard the boat was sour. Danny was still in shock and Amir and Ariadne weren't talking to each other. Isaac had tried to make small talk, but after a general lack of interest from everyone, he decided to stay quiet.

Amir squinted his eyes and looked towards the emerging shape of an island in the distance. 'Look!' he said, standing up and pointing towards the horizon, 'Land ahoy!'

Excited at the thought of escaping the confines of the tiny boat, Danny and Isaac grabbed the oars and began rowing furiously towards the island.

As they neared land, they stopped momentarily to take in the island's landscape. Noting its odd shape, Danny thought for a moment then exclaimed, 'Shoehorn Island!'

He'd heard the fisherman in Highshore talk about it often. Its odd shape meant that all the fish gathered in the bay to escape the strong tides. This allowed the local fishermen to catch them with ease and meant that they were never short of a fish supper.

On reaching the bay, they moored the boat alongside a rickety old dock that reminded Danny of home. As he climbed out, Danny could see Isaac was struggling as he tried to stand on one leg and step up onto the pontoon. Reaching out to him Danny took Isaac's arm and hoisted up before he fell back into the water.

'Thanks,' said Isaac, grinning. 'I'm used to having more legs.'

'Right,' replied Danny, remembering that Isaac was usually half horse, as he watched him waddle away.

Making their way along the pontoon, they could see the vibrant hustle and bustle of the town up ahead. It looked to be a market day with many tradespeople selling their goods from a variety of stalls. The town reminded Danny of home. The same steady pace and peaceful atmosphere. People milled around the marketplace, looking at the wares on offer and buying fresh foods. Despite the familiarity though, Danny was not homesick at all. He actually rather liked the excitement of his new life.

Ariadne was ahead of the group. She walked with confidence and at pace, despite not knowing where they were headed. At the back of the square, she spotted an inn packed with customers streaming through a small circular doorway. As Danny followed Ariadne, trying not to be distracted by the colourful stalls, he wondered what Ariadne's home was like. Was her kingdom grand? Or did she live a humble Royal existence, if there was such a thing? Was her home a stone castle, a marble palace or a huge fort? Danny could hardly believe that another world existed, let alone imagine its finer details. There was so much that he didn't know, but he was keen to find out.

Entering the inn, Ariadne chose a table near the window, and they sat down, but when everyone joined them, the silence from earlier persisted. Danny hadn't realised how hungry he was until the smell of freshly cooked food drifted through his nostrils. He hadn't had a proper homemade meal since long before the pirates took him.

A tough-looking barmaid took their order and slammed five pints of ale down on the table. Danny doubted they were complimentary but didn't dare question the sour-faced host. The meals arrived shortly after and were quickly scoffed, well almost. Amir had turned his nose up at the fish and sulked about, eating his vegetables with a distasteful look. Elda excused this by explaining that they weren't used to fish as they lived in a desert. Ariadne, however, scolded him for loudly making gagging noises. In response he'd shot her a harsh look, clearly still irritated with her. After the plates were cleared, Danny laid out the map on the table and studied it once more.

'So, you said that this was written in ancient elvish?' said Danny looking up at Elda, who already appeared to be translating the strange symbols.

Mumbling to herself, Elda opened a small notebook she'd taken out of her satchel and began to make notes as Danny peered over her shoulder. About ten minutes passed, before Elda put down her pencil with a triumphant smile on her face. She was clearly pleased with herself. She slid the notebook over to Amir, who looked just as proud and, quietly so as not to draw attention to themselves, read Elda's translation out loud…

'That which is lost can always be saved, when hands of great power join at the cave. Only as one will two be free, to claim the gold at the mouth of the sea. This task you cannot complete alone. Fear not, the stars will guide you home.'

'Why does it always have to be written in riddles?' Isaac complained. 'It's never a nice straightforward guide. It never says, 'The treasure's that way!'

'Well, of course not,' snapped Amir, shaking his head. 'If it were that simple, anyone could find it. It has to be written in code so that people like Captain Moreno can't just sail up and take it.'

Ariadne rolled her eyes. Why did he have to be so dismissive? Isaac was only trying to lighten the mood. She never understood why Amir disliked him so much. She was also sceptical of Elda liking Amir. What did she see in him?

'He's right,' chimed in Elda. 'That must be why it's written in elvish, so that humans don't stumble across the map and find Arcadian gold. Think about it, *"hands of great power"* must mean the hands of a Magi.'

Danny was feeling rather overwhelmed. He wanted to save Isabelle, of course he did, but how was he supposed to help her when he knew nothing about the map or Arcadia? He felt useless. Elda could probably figure it all out by herself. He was just tagging along. He didn't even know why they were still helping him. They had no loyalty to him and didn't need his help with the pirates anymore. Maybe they'd be better off without him? No, he thought. He couldn't leave Isabelle. She needed his help. She had told him so and maybe he could bring something to the table from Elda's translation.

'My father used to tell me stories about *"the mouth of the sea,"*' said Danny, who was deep in thought.

'Your bedtime stories aren't going to help us,' snapped Amir.

'How would you know?' responded Ariadne angrily, then turned to Danny, 'What would your father say?'

Danny looked at Amir, waiting to see if he would object. He stayed quiet, so Danny continued. 'he'd say that there was an island so old that it had begun to hollow out. It started as a small cave, and over the years the waves chipped away at the rock. After a few hundred years it was almost a shell. He'd say that when the tide was low, the entrance would open up and ships could sail straight in.'

Danny's eyes teared up slightly. He missed his father. He missed simple things like hearing his voice and listening to all his adventures. He didn't want to cry in front of everyone, so he held back his tears as best he could.

'It's a lovely story,' smiled Ariadne, noticing his obvious discomfort.

Amir rolled his eyes, uninterested in anything that Danny had to say. He was only angry at his sister, but he didn't let that stop him from being rude to everyone. His mood showed no signs of improvement.

'That sounds like great fun,' said Isaac, again attempting to lighten the mood. 'My father never told me stories. I doubt he was creative enough. He's always too serious.'

Danny looked up, subtly wiping his eyes on the back of his sleeve. 'Father used to travel a lot before I was born. He always told me stories about the places he'd visited.'

Elda looked up from her notes and said, 'Do you mean to say that the island was a real place?'

'I'm not sure,' admitted Danny. 'Some of the places were real and some were made up, but it feels like it could be a real place. Maybe the fisherman would know?'

Elda stood up and looked over the map once more. 'I thought *'the mouth of the sea'* was a metaphor,' she said, 'but if the island was a real place, then it could be one of these.' She pointed to the groups of small islands dotted across the map. 'And if so, your father may have come across it on his travels.'

'So, how do we figure out which one it is?' asked Danny as he stared at what must have been fifty or so of the islands.

'No idea,' confessed Elda.

CHAPTER 15

DEAD ENDS

After a peaceful night's sleep at the inn, Ariadne, Elda and Amir met in the dining room for breakfast. Picking up on his idea the night before, Danny and Isaac had gone to look for a local fisherman who may have heard about the *'mouth of the sea'* or a similar place fitting its description. They had asked Amir if he wanted to join them, but he made an excuse to stay with the girls. He wasn't keen on Isaac and hadn't taken to Danny either. Amir's ideal friend would have his strength, intellect and competence. In his opinion, neither Isaac nor Danny had any of these qualities. Amir hadn't yet forgiven Ariadne but decided that he'd rather stay with her and Elda than be stuck with Danny and Isaac.

Elda was on the fence about Danny. He definitely wasn't the hero type they had expected to find on their quest. He didn't know what he was doing half the time and was only motivated by the thought of Isabelle. Elda was the biggest critic when it came to romance. She thought it was a waste of time and certainly not a good enough reason to go on a quest. She knew this was hypocritical and understood all too well what it felt like to love someone that she couldn't be with, but this was different. Danny had a choice and he had chosen a long-winded treasure hunt that wasn't guaranteed to get him the girl. Elda had only met Isabelle once, but something about her didn't sit right. She couldn't put her finger on it, but she felt an odd aura around Isabelle, something she hadn't come across before. Regardless of her personal thoughts, she knew this quest was too important to mess up. It would determine the rest of her life, whether she would become a Shaman or remain Ariadne's companion forever. She loved Ariadne dearly but wanted to follow her own path and make something of herself. A small part of her also hoped that if she could manage to raise her station enough, then maybe she could be with Amir. She pushed this thought to the back of her mind. Unlike Danny, her goals were not centred around a silly love interest. There was an itch at the back of her mind telling her that it would all go wrong and as much as she tried to ignore it, she couldn't help but think Danny would be the reason her plans were ruined. None of that mattered now. They had their task, and they would do their best to complete it and the sooner they got home, the sooner Elda could face the council and discover her fate.

Isaac and Danny had spent the morning looking for anyone who might know the whereabouts of *'the mouth of the sea'*. They had walked the length of Shoehorn Island and spoken to countless people, all of whom laughed at them, saying that there was no such place.

Danny was frustrated. He had been told over and over the island was a myth and yet it was their only lead. He wanted to be helpful. Perhaps Amir and Elda would be nicer to him if he could figure out the next part of the riddle. The fishermen were no help. They were either asking all the wrong people, or they were chasing a dead end. Danny hoped that they would find some answers soon.

While out with Danny, Isaac had spent the morning teaching himself to skip. He had realised early on that he was little use to Danny who seemed to have everything in hand. He thought the town was nice enough, but compared to the busy streets of Osaria, it was dull and uneventful. People milled about with blank expressions on their faces. No one seemed to be smiling or playing or laughing. It was for this reason, that when Isaac had seen a young girl skipping down the street, he busied himself trying to learn. He was now an expert at walking, so he thought it was high time that he learnt something new. Having left Danny wandering along the shore searching for more fisherman, Isaac skipped along feeling quite proud of himself. He wished his father could see him now. Walking around on two legs, hunting for treasure and fighting pirates. He'd be so proud, Isaac thought. He imagined his father galloping up to him after they returned and beaming at his achievements. Deep in thought, it occurred to Isaac that he hadn't actually helped that much. In fact, he'd done quite the opposite. He had given them away to the pirates, resulting in their kidnapping. He had slowed them down in their daily tasks as he learned to walk, and he had no clue how to help them now. Maybe nobody would be proud of him. He slowed his skip to a walk.

After a while the familiar streets melted away and he found himself lost. Great, another thing he had failed at. Which direction had he come from? He wasn't sure. The streets all looked the same and he didn't recognise the dark, peeling buildings or the people who walked past him. He kept walking, peering down alleyways and looking for signs of familiarity. After a while he gave up, frustrated with himself. He knew Amir would scold him for wasting their time when the group would inevitably have to come and find him. He was useless.

Frustrated and fed up, Isaac plonked himself down onto a sturdy barrel outside of a shady bar. Opposite was an old shack-like building. Splintered wooden panels were falling off the walls and the door sagged on its hinges. Above the doorway there was a small, rectangular sign…

Ghost Tours

The shack looked abandoned, and he doubted that anyone actually worked there. To the left of the door, he spotted a tattered flyer that looked like it explained the sights of the ghost tour. Bored, Isaac got up, walked over and picked up the flyer. His eyes flitted down the list of apparently haunted places. It all seemed rather strange to Isaac, whose concept of a ghost was the spirit of his Arcadian ancestors.

He imagined his great aunt, Mildred, sat minding her own business and a tour of people streaming in to watch her. A very odd concept. He had almost finished reading the faded writing when something caught his eye.

'Grand finale,' it read, 'the most haunted place in Renée.' Isaac jumped to his feet as he read the final words, *'the mouth of the sea'.*

Isaac sprinted back to the inn. In his excitement, he'd remembered his way back or perhaps he had just gotten lucky. Either way, he eagerly entered the room, looking around for his friends. He saw them, joined by Danny, sitting at the far end of the room. They looked up as he approached and slammed his hands down on the table, panting to catch his breath.

'Where did you get to?' asked Danny. 'One minute you were there and the next, I turned around and you were gone.'

'Sorry, Danny, I got distracted and wandered off.'

'Of course, you did,' said Elda, shaking her head.

'Let me finish!' insisted Isaac. 'I got lost in the town and ended up on the far side where things were dark and dingy. I wouldn't recommend a visit… except, well, I would actually. There was this old shack and a sign for ghost tours and guess where the final location was…' He waited for some kind answer from the group, but none came so he pushed on with, 'the most haunted place in Renée is called *'the mouth of the sea'.'*

A moment of stunned silence was followed by, 'I knew it wasn't made up!' cried Danny. 'I knew there would be a way to find it!'

'Don't get too excited,' warned Amir. 'We don't know if it's real yet.'

'Oh, for goodness' sake, Amir, don't say that' said Ariadne, glaring at him before turning to smile at Isaac. 'It's the best lead we have. Let's go and see if we can get a tour.'

Isaac led everyone back to the shack where he showed them the sign and pointed out the final location. Elda studied it, turning back to Isaac with an expression that oozed doubt. She tried to look confident but didn't want to get her hopes up.

'So how do we book a tour?' she asked.

'I don't know,' said Isaac.

Amir pushed open the door, which immediately fell off its hinges. Not a good sign, he thought as he stepped inside. The room was dusty and didn't look like it had been in use for many years.

Following him in, Elda created a flame in her palm and held it up. The fire illuminated the tiny room. It was empty apart from a table and a few chairs. On the far wall, hung a large poster, framed in wood. Covered in dust, Amir stepped forward and wiped some of the dust from the glass cover.

'It looks like a map,' he said curiously as he took the frame off the wall and placed it on the table. Using his cloak to wipe away the remaining dust, the image became clearer.

Shoehorn Island was given centre stage. It sat in the middle of the worn parchment, surrounded by other, smaller islands. Five pairs of eager eyes scanned the map, looking for an island named *'the mouth of the sea'*.

'Here!' exclaimed Ariadne, pointing to a tiny speck that could easily be confused with a smudge mark, but on closer inspection proved to be an island due south from Shoehorn. Given its cavernous shape, she was hopeful that this could be the right place and that they would soon have what they needed. 'The island's called Delta.'

'It doesn't look too far away,' responded Elda. 'We could probably make it there before dark.'

'Okay,' said Amir, looking at Isaac with doubt, but trusting Elda's instincts. 'At least we'll know one way or another whether it's a good lead or not.'

They arrived back at the inn with the new map in hand. They packed up their things and, readying themselves for the next leg of their journey, made their way back to the tiny boat, setting off for Delta.

As midday came and went, the sun disappeared behind a bank of threatening dark clouds. The sun was replaced by rumblings of thunder, a biting wind and driving rain that thrashed against their faces. Despite this change in conditions, with Delta only a few miles south of Shoehorn, they'd made good progress and within an hour or so the unique silhouette of the island pierced the gloom and came into view.

'Look!' cried Ariadne, as they drew closer. 'I can see the entrance to a cave!' Her cry was nearly drowned out by the wind.

'Where?' shouted Amir as he tried to shield his eyes from the rain and squint in the direction Ariadne was pointing.

'There, beyond the rocks,' she replied. 'There's a small inlet. You can see the top of the cave. At least I think it's a cave.'

Amir looked again as Danny and Isaac pulled hard on the oars.

'Yes! I can see it!' yelled Amir, his earlier grumpiness replaced by a growing sense of excitement and anticipation. 'But how do we get past the rocks?'

Elda, who was on the tiller at the back of the boat, looked intently through the rain and spotted a narrow passage that appeared to guard the entrance to the cave.

'There!' she cried. The waves rose higher and higher, crashing against the rocks, sending huge plumes of spray into the air and making it almost impossible to see a way through.

Having come this far and with no other leads, they soldiered on, hoping it wouldn't be a wasted journey. Elda shouted out instructions to Danny and Isaac, told Ariadne and Amir to hold tight, and gritted her teeth with a silent prayer as they plunged forward into the waves.

As they entered the passage, the boat rocked side to side, miraculously missing the jagged rocks either side as they tried desperately to keep the boat steady.

To Elda, it seemed as if the weather, which had grown increasingly worse as they'd approached the island, had an almost magical quality to it. Almost as if the storm was protecting the island from unwanted guests. This feeling was reinforced as they broke through the passage and floated freely into the mouth of the cave, where the water became calm, and the wind died down. Thank the gods, thought Elda as she shook the rainwater from her hair.

Everyone's mouths dropped as they looked around the cave. Entering an enormous dome-like cavern, ancient torches lined the walls, the flames casting eerie shadows that danced across the rocky interior. Above them, stalactites hung from the ceiling while, emerging from the water, stalagmites offered a path through to the rear of the cavern where a convenient dock waited for them.

Tying off the boat alongside the dock, they climbed out and stepped onto the rocks. They could see the cave continued over rocky terrain, presumably into the heart of the island.

Danny went over to the wall, where an ornate bracket made of iron held one of the torches. Pulling it out of its housing, he held it up, illuminating the damp walls of the cavern and a seaweed-strewn blanket of rocks which blocked any further path through to the interior of the cave.

'This has to lead somewhere,' said Danny. 'Why else would there be a dock?'

'Perhaps others have been here before,' suggested Isaac.

'Of course, they have,' said Amir, shaking his head. 'But there doesn't seem to be anything here, so we need to try and find a way through.'

'Absolutely,' said Danny. 'There's no time to waste.' He ran forward and, like a gazelle, leapt up onto the nearest rock, clambering up and disappearing out of sight. He was clearly excited, and with the others following his lead, they reached the top in no time. Looking out over a plateau of relatively even rocks, Danny could see a faint glow in the distance. The air was thick with salt and Danny recognized the familiar smell of crab and mussels. Carefully wandering over the slippery surface, he kept walking until the rocky floor gave way to sand.

He stopped at the edge, turning around and waiting for the others to join him. Looking back, Danny could see Isaac struggling to balance on the slippery rocks, but with Ariadne's help he managed to stay on his feet. In front of them, Amir and Elda reached Danny's side.

'Gods!' exclaimed Elda as they reached the edge. A shallow rock pool full of intricate shells and tiny, colourful fish stretched out in front of them. The pool was brimming with life, odd for a seemingly deserted cave, but it wasn't the bustling creatures that caused Elda's reaction.

The water was glowing softly with a bioluminescence that made it look like the starry night sky.

'Wow!' exclaimed Ariadne and Isaac in sync. It was a beautiful sight that captivated everyone as they stared, mesmerized by the water.

'It is beautiful,' said Elda softly, glancing at the others, 'but look around. It's a dead end.'

CHAPTER 16

A GOLDEN OPPORTUNITY

Danny sat with his head in his hands. They had failed. This was their only lead and it had resulted in a dead end. He would never free Isabelle and never find out what happened to his father. He was out of luck.

Elda was slumped against the cavern wall. What were they going to do now? she thought. She would be a laughingstock when they returned home, and she had no hope of being a Shaman. How hard could it be to find some old treasure? And yet they were at a loss. With only a day left, they had no hope of finishing their trial successfully.

Isaac and Ariadne spoke softly to one another, looking over the two maps and comparing notes. They too were disappointed but were trying to think of ways to salvage the situation. Amir, on the other hand, was frustratedly kicking stones at the water's edge. He had told them that this was a waste of time, but nobody listened. And now they were out of time and out of ideas. He threw a pebble into the water, which splashed and shimmered with light. The splash rippled across the water, dying as it reached the shore. What would happen when they returned? he wondered. Would his father be disappointed? He thought it foolish that he had to partake in the trials to begin with. The trials determined what career a young person might have, but Amir's future was already decided. He was a Prince: he would marry a Princess and raise Royal babies who would run rampant around Osaria. He would have no real worries or responsibilities and would never struggle for money. He was content in this and, in his frustration, regretted joining the trials to begin with.

He threw another rock. This time he threw it up and it hit the side of the cave. He grabbed a handful more and began aiming, seeing how far he could throw them. He looked to his hand to choose his next victim, when something caught his eye. In his palm, surrounded by rocks and covered in sand, was a golden coin. He reached into the water, washing the sand from the piece. Pressed into its face was the same symbol as seen on the map. He held it up and called to Ariadne.

'I think you dropped this,' he said. 'Not that it's much use now.'

Everyone looked over, trying to figure out what Amir had found. Ariadne opened her bag searching for her coin and after a minute, pulled it out triumphantly. 'That's not my coin,' she said with excitement. 'Where did you find that?'

Amir was shocked. He suddenly realised what this meant. 'If it's not your coin…' he paused and scanned the ground looking for any other gold pieces. 'Then we *are* in the right place. This *is* where Xander hid his treasure!'

'Let me see it,' said Elda, holding out her hand.

Amir gave the coin to her, and she studied it carefully. 'I think you're right,' she laughed.

Excitement filled the cave. The coin was passed around, and once they were all convinced, they set about trying to find more. Everyone got down on their hands and knees and began digging. After a few minutes, and no more coins, the group sat up looking puzzled. Danny got to his feet, looked round the cave and peered into the water. He couldn't see much through the bioluminescence, so decided to wade in to get a better view. Isaac followed his lead, and soon they were all paddling about in the shallow water.

'Here!' shouted Elda, holding up another coin.

'And here!' whooped Ariadne, lifting another out of the water.

'Look at this,' said Isaac beckoning the others to join him alongside the back wall of the rock pool. He was tugging seaweed and debris clear of a curious rectangular shaped rock, half submerged in the water and resting against the wall.

Danny waded further into the now waist deep salty water and joined Isaac.

'This rock is far too neat to be natural,' he said. 'It looks like it's been carved by hand and just left there. 'What do you think it is, Danny?'

'I'm not sure,' he replied. 'Here, help me lift it,' as he bent down and wrapped his arms round the rock.

Isaac followed suit and between them they managed to lift it out of the water and placed it to one side of the pool.

'Look,' said Danny pointing at a large X carved into the face of the rock.

'X for Xander,' suggested Isaac.

'Or X marks the spot," he replied.

As the others waded in to join them, they gathered around the stone and speculated as to the meaning of the symbol. Elda had an idea.

'Amir, can you help me up?' she asked. He stepped forward and steadied her as she climbed onto a ledge that had previously been hidden from view. From her perch, she placed her hand on the wall for support and looked down into the water, hoping a new perspective would lead to another clue. Danny had the same plan and with Isaac's help joined Elda on the ledge. Narrower than he expected, Danny too reached out to the wall for support, but instead accidentally put his hand over Elda's.

'Sorry,' he apologised and tried to pull his hand away.

'Get off,' complained Elda when his hand didn't move.

'I can't move it!'

'What do you mean, "you can't move it,"' she said, as she tried to slide her hand out from under his.

'It's stuck!'

'Don't be ridiculous!' she cried, but no matter how hard they both tried, neither hand would budge from the wall.

'Wait!' Ariadne shouted over the bickering couple. 'The writing on the map! It said something about powerful hands joining at the cave! Maybe this is supposed to happen!'

Elda didn't look convinced but placed her other hand against the wall then glared at Danny. 'Go on, you too,' she said looking down at his other hand.

The moment all four hands were in place, the wall began to ripple just as water might ripple at the touch of a stone. Both looked at each other as their hands disappeared into the wall.

'What's happening?' cried Danny, as he felt the wall drawing them in still further.

'It's some form of portal,' said Elda and although she was used to such things, even she was on the verge of panic as she was unable to pull back.

'Lean back,' shouted Ariadne.

'We're trying!' They both yelled in response, but instead their words were lost as Danny and Elda were suddenly sucked into the wall and disappeared as it closed behind them, leaving Ariadne, Isaac and Amir alone in the cave.

Scrabbling up onto the ledge, all three pushed against the wall, but it was no use, they couldn't get through. They tried calling Elda and Danny, but no response came. Climbing back down into the pool, they busied themselves looking for another way through.

'What do you think happened?' asked Isaac, still shocked from what he'd just seen.

'At a guess,' said Ariadne, 'I think our quest has just moved on a step further forward.'

'So, what happens now?' asked Amir.

'I guess we'll just have to wait,' shrugged Ariadne, 'and hope they come back safely.'

'With the gold,' said Amir.

'Yes, Amir, with the gold.'

On the other side of the wall, Danny and Elda had landed in shallow water and were soaked through. The room was cold and when Elda turned around to see where they were, she could hardly believe her eyes. They were in another cavern, this one twice the size of the last. The ceiling was high and an opening in the roof let in plenty of light. Elda tapped Danny on the shoulder, but he was busy patting the wall and trying to push back through.

Danny,' she said, barely able to contain the excitement in her voice. 'Turn around.'

Danny stopped pushing and turned around… 'Woah!' he whispered under his breath as he used a hand to shield his eyes from a bombardment of shimmering lights and reflections that bounced off the walls of the cavern.

As his eyes adjusted to the change in lighting, he gazed around the cavern and marvelled at the wall-to-wall abundance of golden jewels, baubles, ornaments and coins all set amidst a wealth of treasures beyond anything he could possibly imagine.

'Isn't it amazing?' said Elda, the awe in her voice as transparent as the jewels on which her eyes settled.

Danny nodded in agreement. He pointed to the centre of the cavern where a large stone plinth stood, with a red velvet cushion resting upon it. Upon this, a golden crown of such delicate intricacy and beauty sat poised and awaiting an audience. It glistened brightly, leaving them both speechless. In silence, they took a minute to soak in the glorious scenery.

'It's beautiful, isn't it,' said Elda. 'It reminds me of an ancient elven design. Come on, let's take a closer look.'

With that, they made their way carefully towards the plinth, stopping here and there in wonderment and disbelief at the sheer volume of treasure that filled the cavern. Careful not to damage anything, they eventually arrived at the Crown's resting place.

Danny reached out his hand to touch...

'Wait!' said Elda, pointing to a scroll of parchment protruding from a recess in the plinth beneath the velvet cushion.

Danny's hand changed direction and instead carefully took hold of the scroll and gently eased it from the recess. Held together with a maroon silk ribbon, there was a single name written along its edge... ADANION... 'Xander's left a message for his son,' exclaimed Danny. 'Perhaps he's left the treasure for him too?'

'Who knows,' said Elda, turning her attention to the crown. Examining it carefully, she could see it was beautifully crafted in Arcadian gold and what's more, the rim was lined with ancient elvish inscriptions. The words were so old and worn that Elda could barely read them let alone translate them. But there was one word, repeated many times, that Elda knew all too well, Delos.

'Well, should we read it?' asked Danny, interrupting her thoughts.

'No, it's not for us,' she replied decisively as she took the scroll from Danny's hand and placed it in her bag.

'How much of this do you think you'll need to buy Isabelle's freedom?' she asked, changing the subject before he could object.

Admittedly, Danny didn't have a clue. They had been in such a rush the night of the escape that he hadn't asked for specifics. The captain would want all of the gold, that was for sure, but there was no way that they could carry this much. Instead, Danny filled his pockets and bag with as much gold as he could carry, hoping it would be enough. Elda did the same, beginning first with the crown. She placed it carefully in her bag.

'Come on,' she said, 'we'd better get out of here. We've already disturbed this ancient place enough.' She turned to pick her way back through the treasure trove to the cavern wall where she gave it a good shove with both hands, but nothing happened.

'I think we have to do it together,' said Danny as he joined her and held up his hands.

Taking a deep breath, they stepped forward, placed their hands on the wall and pushed, not that they needed to for as soon as their hands came together, the wall rippled and before they knew it, found themselves back on the ledge looking out into an empty cavern.

'Where have the others gone?' asked Danny.

'They're probably waiting for us at the boat,' said Elda. 'At least I hope they are.'

'Fingers crossed,' said Danny as, with pockets jingling and bags swinging, they made their way back through the rock pool and across the plateau of slippery rocks.

Reaching the final large rock, they clambered up and slid down the other side towards the boat.

'You'll never guess what we found!' shouted Danny as he landed, but instead of a reply, he felt a hand grasp the back of his collar and yank him off his feet. Kicking frantically in the air, he pushed away from his attacker and spun round to see Elda in the grip of one of the pirates from the Hellbourne Princess. In shock, Danny stood still and was once again grabbed by his pirate assailant.

'Oh, I think I could probably guess,' sneered the deep voice of Captain Moreno, who leant against the cave's cold wall. 'What do you think, my dear?' he asked, turning to Isabelle, who was standing by his side.

'I can only imagine,' she spoke softly as Danny, deflated from his earlier euphoria, looked towards the dock where the others were back in the boat, gagged and bound and all looking thoroughly miserable.

CHAPTER 17

TRICKS OF THE TRADE

Melanie and a handful of crew mates grabbed Elda and Danny and tried dragging them to the boats. As they struggled to free themselves, coins fell out of their pockets and more pirates rushed in to pick them up. Their swords were taken, and their bags searched. How had this happened? Danny thought. Had Isabelle lead them here? In his frustration, tears built up behind his eyes. He felt betrayed.

Moreno smiled at him in triumph as he was brought down off the rocks and thrown at the captain's feet. Melanie kept a tight grip on Danny's shoulder and two more escorted Elda to the boat where she was tied up with the others.

'Thank you for this, Danny,' smirked the captain. 'We couldn't have done it without you.'

Elda's bag was handed to the captain, who looked inside

eagerly, retrieved the crown and placed it on his head.

'It doesn't really suit you,' grumbled Danny.

Greasy locks spilled down Moreno's shoulders which, when combined with his gold tooth and rugged clothes, looked completely out of keeping with the beautiful golden crown.

'Silence, boy!' he snapped back.

Danny ignored him and turned to Isabelle. 'How could you do this?' he pleaded, his voice cracking as he tried his best to hold back the tears. 'I was trying to help you.'

'You have helped me.' she replied quietly, her head bowed.

'Look at me,' demanded Danny, 'why?'

Isabelle slowly lifted her head. Tears were running down her cheeks. 'I don't need anything more from you, Danny...' She paused to wipe them away. 'Why would I run away when I have everything I've ever wanted right here?' Her voice was steady and despite the conviction in her voice, tears continued to drip down her face.

'Ha!' laughed the captain. 'You were just a means to an end, Danny Boy.'

Danny could feel his own tears now running freely down his

face. 'You're his slave, Isabelle. You must see that. You should have stuck to our plan. You would be so much better off with us.'

Moreno laughed again, so loudly it echoed around the cavern. 'You really think she'd rather be with you? I have riches. I have ships and I have a loyal crew. What have you got to offer her?'

'Freedom,' said Danny, the simplicity of his statement making it all the more powerful as his eyes locked on Isabelle's. 'All the gold in the world, all the ships in the oceans and all the crew...' He looked round with contempt at the captain's ragtag band of followers and shook his head. 'All that could never replace being free. Being able to do what you want, when you want and be with who...' His voice broke as Isabelle let out a soft cry.

'Oh, how touching,' mocked the captain. 'So, you think the two of you will sail off into the sunset and live happily ever after?' The crew laughed as the captain walked over to Isabelle. He held her face in his hand and lifted her chin. 'And what about you, my dear? Do you love him?'

Danny looked at her hopelessly. 'Please,' he begged.

She looked away, her eyes turning to the captain. 'I feel nothing,' she said, tears blubbering from her eyes.

'You see,' laughed the captain. 'You're just a fishmonger from a small town and you will never be anything more.'

'I'd rather be a fishmonger than a fool of a pirate like you,' he snarled and tried to lunge at Moreno, who took a step back as Danny was hauled backwards off his feet by his captors.

'Well, maybe it's time to teach you a lesson when we're back on board,' responded the captain, the look of amusement no longer on his face as he caressed the handle of a cat o' nine tails that hung loosely by his side, 'and then we'll see who's the fool.'

As these events were unfolding, Ariadne was hatching a plan. The guards had taken their swords and her bow but had missed a tiny knife she kept hidden inside her belt. With her hands tied behind her back, she managed to twist her belt around and, with Danny offering the perfect distraction, she elbowed Amir alongside her and gestured for him to look behind them.

Amir looked over his shoulder and saw the knife in her hands.

'Psst!' he hissed quietly to the others through his gag.

Bound back-to-back, Elda and Isaac turned, and Amir nodded his head down towards Ariadne's hands. Instantly sticking their hands out behind them, they stretched their bonds tight allowing Ariadne to start cutting through them one by one.

It took a while, but eventually they were free, and she passed the knife to Elda, who cut the remaining bonds around Ariadne's wrists.

'What's the plan?' Isaac whispered, his gag muffling his voice.

Elda pulled off her gag. 'There is no plan.' She grinned and with a blood curdling battle cry leapt forward and grabbed her sword from the pile of weapons in the well of the boat. Taking their lead from Elda, the others followed suit as they reached for their weapons, jumped out of the boat and charged at the pirates.

Captain Moreno spun round as the sound of their battle cries bounced off the walls of the cavern. Realising they were under attack, he yelled, 'Get them, lads!' and stepped back as his crew rushed forward.

As Elda, Amir, Isaac and Ariadne engaged the crew and an almighty battle ensued, Danny could see they were outnumbered three to one and knew he had to help. Lifting his foot, he suddenly leant back, raked his heel down the front of Melanie's shins and thrust his head back catching her full on the nose, causing her to let him go and lose her balance. He spun round and reached for her sword. She recovered quickly—this wasn't the first scrap she'd been in. Melanie pivoted away from Danny and with a huge grin, wiped a dribble of blood from her damaged nose with the back of her hand and pulled her sword free of its sheath.

As is so often the case in moments of danger, human nature comes up with two options, fight or flight, and in this instant, Danny chose the former as he dived forward taking out Melanie's legs and sending her flying through the air and into the water.

'I can't swim!' she screamed as she struggled to keep her head above water.

Jumping to his feet Danny grabbed her sword and looked down at her. 'A pirate who can't swim!' He laughed as he watched her grab hold of one of the boat's edges and ran to help the others.

Despite the difference in numbers, it was clear to Danny that his friend's skill and fighting ability meant they were holding their own, so instead of joining them he looked out for Moreno.

'There!' shouted Elda above the noise of clashing swords and the screams of the wounded pirates, as she pointed towards the dock. 'Don't let him get away, Danny!'

Moreno, still wearing the crown and with the bags of gold hanging from each shoulder, was staggering along the dock towards the boat. Racing forward, Danny shouldered past two pirates, sending them crashing into the water, and quickly caught up with the captain.

'Not so fast!' he shouted as the captain was about to lob the bags into the boat.

Moreno turned, dropped the bags and drew his cutlass.

'Never took you for a coward, Moreno,' said Danny.

Moreno let out a growl and slowly took off the crown and placed it carefully on top of a nearby rock. 'You'll regret that, boy, when I slice you in two and send you down to the bottom of the ocean!'

As Moreno lunged forward, Danny managed to dodge his thrust. As their swords met for the first time with a resounding crash, he realised he had never fought anyone as strong as the captain before. Struggling to hold on, he stepped back and swept Moreno's sword away from him. He repeated this move time and time again as they jumped to and fro until, both exhausted, they stood facing each other, taking in huge gulps of air to catch their breath.

Meanwhile, Elda took full advantage of her magic and threw jinxes in all directions as she and Amir slashed through pirate after pirate. One scrawny-looking woman ended up stuck to the floor, unable to move her feet. Another two crewmates found themselves tied together and suspended from the cave's ceiling. Ariadne's tactics proved equally effective. She perched on the rocks, shooting at the oncoming pirates with her bow. She aimed for their hands and feet, meaning that they couldn't hold their swords, and it would make it harder for them to charge at anyone else. Isaac too, was good with his sword, but was disadvantaged as unused to fighting in human form. His style developed into pushing and shoving pirates into the water, which proved to be surprisingly effective. It took so long for them to crawl back up and across the rocks, they were exhausted by the time they reached the top, not to mention soaking wet. Just as he was beginning to enjoy himself, he spotted an archer creeping across the higher rocks, aiming his bow down towards Amir.

'No!' screamed Isaac as he barged past two pirates, pushing one into another and sending them tumbling down the rocks. Unable to hear Isaac's warning, Amir continued to fight on as the archer released his arrow. Too late to push Amir out of the way, Isaac leapt into the air as the arrow, heading for Amir's heart, plunged deep into Isaac's shoulder. He fell to the ground.

'Elda!' screamed Amir as he threw another pirate to one side and rushed to Isaac's side.

Seeing Isaac lying on the floor and knowing he was hurt, Elda rushed to help him as Ariadne fired an arrow at the archer, hitting him in the chest and sending him flying from his perch into the water. With most of the pirates now floundering in the water, yelling in pain as they held their injured arms and legs, Ariadne looked towards the dock.

Having recovered his breath, Captain Moreno moved menacingly forward, sword raised and with a furious look on his face. He backed Danny to the edge of the rocks. Moreno laughed and began to swing his sword down towards Danny's head. Danny saw this coming and side-stepped out of Moreno's downwards range. Moreno switched his point of attack and slashed across Danny's arm, causing him to drop his sword.

Seemingly oblivious to his crew's demise, Moreno laughed and stepped forward holding the point of his sword at Danny's throat.

'Time to meet your maker, lad!' he crowed, but as he raised his sword for the final blow, an arrow from Ariadne's bow whistled through the air and buried itself into the back of his hand. He dropped the sword, yelling in pain, 'Arrgh!' Danny's eyes opened wide in delight as he leapt forward, shoulder-charged Moreno out of the way, grabbed the fallen sword and plunged it deep into the pirate captain's stomach.

Looking down aghast, Moreno was barely able to comprehend what had just happened. He sank to his knees, clasped his wound with both hands and looked up at Danny. 'It can't be,' he grunted.

'See you in the next life' responded Danny as he raised his foot, pushing Moreno backwards. He watched as the pirate captain fell over the edge of the rocks and into the water, floating for a few moments before disappearing into the darkness.

Overcome with exhaustion and with the adrenalin draining from his body, Danny took one final look into the water, just to be sure, then fell to his knees. Ariadne watched him from across the water, relieved at the captain's demise. Amir was alongside her with his sword to Melanie's throat and Elda was crouched over Isaac. Danny took a deep breath, hauled himself to his feet and hobbled over to them.

'Is he okay?' Danny asked, the concern in his voice evident as he reached the group and looked down at Isaac.

Isaac opened his eyes and looked up at Danny. 'Just a scratch,' he said, promptly fainting as Elda snapped off the shaft and bandaged around the arrow.

'We'll leave that in there for now,' said Elda. 'We don't want to cause any more damage by pulling it out until we find a doctor.'

'But he'll be alright, won't he?' asked Danny.

'He'll be fine,' she replied. 'If nothing else, he's a tough old centaur.'

'Okay, then. So, what are we going to do with this lot?' he asked, looking round at what was left of the pirates, all of whom— well, at least those who hadn't retreated—had lost the will to fight having witnessed the demise of their Captain. 'You can let her go,' said Danny, calling out to Amir who still had hold of Melanie.

'Shouldn't we keep her as a hostage?' said Amir, clearly reluctant to let her go.

'And do what with her?' said Ariadne. 'She knows she's

defeated and besides, I can't see her having anything more to do with our quest.'

'Good point,' said Amir, who decided he wouldn't have known what to do with her anyway.

Releasing her from his grip, Amir watched as Melanie grabbed her sword and made her way towards the dock, but not before a nod of thanks to Danny as she passed him by. With a final look at the water where Moreno had disappeared, she reached down for the captain's hat that lay masterless on the dock, gathered what was left of the crew together and climbed aboard one of the boats.

Danny watched as they put out the oars and began rowing towards the mouth of the cave and no doubt the Hellbourne Princess beyond, a ship he hoped never to see again.

'What did I miss?' said Isaac as he woke and tried to sit up.

Amir knelt down and placed a gentle hand on his good shoulder. 'Thank you for saving me back there. I owe you my life.' He bowed his head. 'I will be forever in your debt.'

Isaac looked thrilled with this compliment and promptly replied with, 'All in a day's work for Arcadia's best centaur.' He grinned, though he looked as though he may soon faint again.

'He won't ever let you forget that in a hurry,' laughed Elda.

'I know,' smiled Amir, 'and when I get the chance, I'll make sure Father knows I was saved by Arcadia's Greatest Centaur.'

Throughout the entire battle, just one person had remained silent and still and it was her they turned to next.

'So, what are we going to do about her?' asked Ariadne, gesturing towards Isabelle, who was looking into the depths towards where Moreno's body had disappeared. Realising she was now the centre of attention, she looked up and saw them watching her.

'I think that should be up to Danny,' said Elda.

Ariadne and Amir nodded in agreement and looked at Danny.

'She stays with us,' said Danny. He couldn't bring himself to look her in the eye, but there was more to the denial of her feelings towards him. 'We have a lot to talk about, but for now I think we should return to the inn. I don't know about you, but I could do with some rest, and we need to get Isaac to a doctor.

With everyone in agreement, they gathered the gold and safely stored the crown in Elda's satchel, then loaded everything into the boat in readiness for their journey back to Shoehorn. Before they left, Elda led the Arcadians in a small prayer for the fallen soldiers. It was a nice gesture, Danny thought as he stood quietly, watching.

Leaving the cave behind, the sun slowly dipped below the horizon. A glorious shade of orange was soon replaced by a crystal-clear night sky dotted with pinpricks of light as if the heavens looked down upon the intrepid adventurers. They had finished their task, thought Ariadne, and soon the Arcadians would head home and Danny... Well, that was something to be discussed in the morning after a well-deserved night's rest.

CHAPTER 18

BLURRED VISION

As the sun rose again over Shoehorn, the streets began to fill with people. The island's morning routine was like clockwork, as the same people went about their same daily activities, at the same relaxed pace. Danny watched them out of his bedroom window, glad of the familiar scenes. He thought again how similar Shoehorn was to Highshore. He loved his home, but was glad that he had left, even if it had been as a result of being kidnapped. The last few weeks had been the most exciting of his life and he had no plans to return to his seaside home. Perhaps he would find another adventure, or even just a new place to explore.

Isaac yawned from his bed and groaned at Danny for opening the curtains. They'd found a doctor as soon as they got back to the island the night before. It had been late, and he wasn't happy at being called from his bed, but he was a kind soul and removed the arrowhead from Isaac's shoulder, cauterised the wound, replaced the bandages and gave him something to relieve the pain and help him sleep. Whatever they had given him must have been strong. He'd slept like a baby and no sooner had Isaac woken up; he'd fallen back to sleep. By the time Danny was dressed and ready to leave the room, Isaac was snoring merrily once more. As his legs twitched under the covers, Danny guessed he was no doubt dreaming of galloping across a faraway field.

Danny and Amir headed downstairs where they joined the girls in the dining room for breakfast. Ariadne and Elda sat across from Isabelle and had clearly been grilling her for a while. Ariadne looked up as they walked over, nudging Elda to alert her of their presence.

'Maybe you can get something out of her, Danny,' sighed Elda. 'She won't say a word to either of us.' Ariadne and Elda got up and indicated for Amir to join them at a new table.

Isabelle sat with her head bowed and her hands in her lap as Danny took a seat opposite her. The awkward silence remained for a few minutes before he gathered his words.

'I hope you've got a really good reason for betraying me,' he said softly.

'I didn't have a choice,' she replied.

'You always have a choice, Isabelle. We all have a choice in the world, even when things seem impossible.'

Her bottom lip trembled, and she began to sob. 'You don't understand.'

'You're right, I don't understand.' He was still furious at her betrayal, but he knew that it would do no good to show it if he wanted answers, so he kept his tone soft. 'But I want to understand, so please tell me, Isabelle.'

'I wasn't lying before,' she said. 'Moreno owned me, but not in the way you think.' She cleared her throat. 'Years ago, when Moreno first found the map, he went searching for the treasure. He couldn't find it, because he didn't understand the inscriptions, but he knew they were written in elvish. He knew that without an elvish speaker he would have no chance at finding the gold, so he went looking for one. He found my sister and I, when I was working as a fortune teller on a small island called Bruano.'

'But you're not an elvish speaker. Are you?'

'Moreno knew that many Arcadians, in the mortal world, used their powers to make a living. Circus acts are the most common cover.'

'So, you're a Magi?'

'No, I'm a seer. Born of the Shaman clan. My ancestors were the prophets of old. Nowadays, very few Shaman have the gift and even fewer learn to master it.'

'And you're one of those few?'

'Yes, and because of that, Moreno tracked me down and asked me to help him. I refused at first, but...' Her eyes filled with tears. 'He took my sister and told me that the only way to get her back was to help him find the treasure.'

Danny sat back in his seat and although he felt desperately sorry for Isabelle, he was still struggling with her betrayal.

'So why did you need me? I'm not elvish and it was a long time after I was kidnapped that we came across Elda and her friends, and besides, if you can translate the writing then why did you need us?'

'I saw it,' she said, wiping away her tears. 'I saw it in a vision. We had been searching for almost two years. I had translated the elvish, but that only got us halfway there. We found the cave, but we couldn't get through the wall. We had all but given up when I had a vision of you.'

'What kind of vision?'

'You were in Highshore. Then you were on board the ship, and then I saw you and her—' She gestured to Elda. '—in the chamber, with all the gold. You were wearing the crown. You have to understand Danny, everything I did was to save my sister.'

'I do, Isabelle,' said Danny, his anger evaporating and being replaced instead with a feeling of guilt. Isabelle had, after all, done what anyone would do to protect their family.

'I really didn't mean to hurt you, Danny. If it's any consolation, at least now you know who your father is.'

'What?' exclaimed Danny. 'What do you mean?'

'Haven't you figured it out?' Isabelle was surprised. 'The crown. In my vision you were wearing the crown, Xander's crown. The Crown of Delos, meant for his son. I can't be sure, but I think it's meant for you, Danny. Or, as I should say, Adanion.' She reached into her bag and pulled out a blue leather journal. She slid it across the table, offering it to Danny.

'No, I can't be,' said Danny, shaking his head. 'My father was a sailor and he…'

'Vanished,' said Isabelle, cutting him off.

'Yes, he left to join the Navy, but he was just an ordinary man,' insisted Danny, a little too loudly for their conversation to remain private.

Concerned for Danny, Ariadne, Elda and Amir walked over to see what the commotion was about and, with a nod of agreement from him, Isabelle told them of her theory. Danny sat quietly, still stunned at her words. Hearing them a second time did not help them sink in.

'Please tell me that's not possible,' begged Danny as he looked imploringly from Elda to Ariadne and back again.

They were just as stunned as he was. Could it be possible? thought Elda. She wasn't sure. Delos were very secretive about many things, and it wouldn't surprise her if they had many hidden truths. But this was something of such importance. She didn't know how it could have been kept secret for all these years. How could Danny be related to the Delos royals? And why was he wearing their crown in Isabelle's vision? It was hard to believe. She had to admit to Danny, 'I simply don't know.'

Ariadne stood, deep in thought. She remembered the words her father had spoken to her before she left. He had said that Osaria was in danger and that only a miracle could save them. What if this was that miracle? Neither she nor Elda knew for sure, but what she did know was that if the theory was true, it could alter the fate of her kingdom.

Danny opened the journal that Isabelle had given him. The pages opened naturally near the centre where a single page had been torn out. Ariadne took the map from her shoulder and opened the tube. She fished out the loose letter that Xander had written and placed it on top of the journal. The pages fit together like a glove.

'So, this was his journal?' asked Danny.

'Yes,' replied Isabelle. 'I took it from the captain's quarters. I also put that page in with the map. I thought you might figure it out yourselves.'

Danny flicked through the pages to the front of the book. There were hundreds of handwritten notes and sketches, all detailing Xander's adventures. On the inside page, scrawled in black ink, was the writer's full name. 'Alexander Blake,' Danny read aloud.

'Isn't he the Venator warrior who kidnapped Princess Leonora?' asked Ariadne.

'I've heard about him, too,' added Amir. 'Melbourne goes on and on about him in our combat lessons.'

'Who is he?' asked Danny, looking worried.

'The story goes,' said Amir, 'that he was Venator's greatest fighter and that he went rogue and kidnapped Delos' future Queen just days before her coronation. Her brother Lykos then hunted them down and killed him... but not before he killed the Princess.'

'Don't say that!' butted in Ariadne. 'There's so many stories about Delos and Venator and none of them are proven. That story could be a million miles from the truth.'

'But it could be true?' asked Danny.

'Let's not think about that for now,' said Elda trying to reassure him.

'So how do we find out if he really is my father?' asked Danny. He directed this question at Elda as he thought, out of everyone, she'd have the best answer.

To his surprise, it was Isabelle who offered the answer. 'It's simple. You go to Arcadia and face the council.'

'What council? Who are they and what makes you think they know anything about my father?'

'The Council of Elders, Danny,' explained Ariadne. 'They know everything about the history of our world, so if anyone knows it would be them.'

'I think she's right,' said Elda as she looked at Isabelle, 'which means we must return to Arcadia with Danny.'

As they all took a moment to take in this momentous turn of events, Isaac clomped down the stairs, yawning as he walked into the breakfast room. "What did I miss?' he asked for the second time in twenty-four hours and plonked himself down at the table.

Elda sighed and Ariadne giggled as for the final time Isabelle told the story that could very well change the history of their world.

As Isabelle finished and with Elda having had time to think, she announced their next steps. They were taking Danny back to Arcadia to find out if he really was a Grigori. That much was obvious and, while the Arcadians were all in agreement that this was the right call, Danny on the other hand wasn't so sure. He was extremely nervous, but knowing his fate was hanging in the balance, he knew he had no choice but to join his new friends and travel to a whole new realm.

After packing up their belongings, they donned their cloaks and stepped outside. Elda found a quiet spot by the docks where they checked the coast was clear and formed a small circle with Danny following Ariadne's lead.

'Is everyone ready?' asked Ariadne, removing an orb from the hilt of her dagger. Met with nods of approval, she crushed the orb between her fingers and watched as a red shiny liquid fell to the floor then began to swirl round and round, slowly at first, then faster and faster, weaving itself upwards until a portal formed in front of them.

'After you,' grinned Ariadne as Elda entered the portal, closely followed by Amir, Isaac and Isabelle and finally...

'I promise it's safe,' said Ariadne as she took hold of Danny's hand.

Danny had always thought of himself as brave, but faced with an interdimensional portal, he doubted his strength. It was one thing fighting pirates and exploring new places in the human world, but a whole new realm? He was scared. He thought about Highshore, wondering if he would ever see it again.

Saying goodbye to his old life and stepping into a completely new one brought sweet sorrow, but he knew that he would regret it if he didn't take the leap. So, with a final look around at the mortal world, he held his breath and

stepped through the portal.

CHAPTER 19

ARCADIA

Beams of light hit Danny's face. He let go of Ariadne and held his hands out in front of his eyes, squinting to try and make out the scene unfolding in front of him. He saw the outlines of hundreds of people circling round and round them like churning water. The sharp ringing noise that surrounded him faded away, replaced instead by the sound of cheering and chants from a crowd as he emerged from the portal.

Ariadne was the last to step through and the portal quickly closed behind her with a flash of light. Danny looked around slowly, taking in the scenery. The six of them—Team Kiba, Danny and Isabelle—were standing in the centre of a large colosseum crammed full of spectators. Danny hadn't known what to expect, but this

Dramatic entrance was not what he had imagined.

The open-air stadium was carved out of beige sandstone. It was old and crumbling and yet, masked by the crowd, looked bright and colourful. Beyond the stone walls, Danny could see rows of trees, stretching back across the skyline. To his left, the dusty red rooftops of a huge city were dominated by a glorious palace. The dome at its centre was of royal blue, with a pattern of intricate gold metalwork and jewels that sparkled in the sunlight.

As Danny marvelled at the spectacle around him, a cacophony of trumpets echoed around the colosseum heralding the arrival of... Danny looked round expecting to see a resplendent entourage of perhaps chariots of gold and colourful characters. Instead, an elderly man dressed in a scruffy brown tunic and leather overcoat approached a wooden stage in the centre of the arena. Diminutive in stature, he had a pair of small round eyeglasses balanced on the end of a large red nose. He reminded Danny of one of the fishermen from Highshore, skin cracked and clothes rugged and full of wisdom and stories.

Danny guessed this man's appearance was the least interesting thing about him. As he mounted a short flight of steps and walked to the centre of the stage, the crowd hushed, and he cleared his throat.

'Who's he?' whispered Danny.

'Professor Burmir,' replied Ariadne.

As Danny looked at her, his eyes opened wide in surprise. She looked different. The differences were subtle, but definitely there. Her face was thinner, her eyes were bigger, her ears were pointed. Her limbs looked daintier than before, and she seemed to glow ever so slightly.

'And that's Melbourne,' she said, pointing to a huge figure of a man coming into view from behind the stage. For a moment, Danny wondered how he could be so tall then saw the lower half of his body wasn't human. From the waist down he had the body of a horse and Danny realised he must be a centaur.

'Woah,' he said under his breath.

'Pretty impressive, eh?'

Danny jumped and looked round. Isaac stood behind him, or perhaps 'towered above him' would be a better description. Isaac, too, had transformed.

He no longer appeared to be an average sized human, with slightly disproportionate leg muscles. He now looked grand and proud. He must have been at least three foot taller than Danny. His hind legs were dark brown and well groomed. He looked majestic, which was not a word Danny ever thought he would use to describe Isaac. He was amazed.

'Welcome back, Team Kiba!' announced Professor Burmir, his voice resonating around the colosseum. 'Well done for completing your trial within the time limit…'

He clearly had a whole speech planned and was ready to congratulate them all, but he was interrupted by Melbourne's booming voice. 'Who are they?' His accent was thick and intimidating as it vibrated around the stadium.

Realising Melbourne was referring to him and Isabelle, Danny took her hand and stepped back, hoping to hide behind Isaac's hindquarters.

The silence that followed was worse than Melbourne's question. Danny felt the eyes of every Arcadian fall upon them, an awkward tension that seemed to last forever.

'They're with us!' called out Ariadne, stepping forward to stand between Danny, Isabelle and Melbourne.

'Princess Ariadne,' scorned Melbourne. 'You know better than anyone, it is forbidden to bring mortals here. Explain yourself.'

'They're not humans,' she responded firmly. 'At least, we don't *think* they are.'

Melbourne trotted forward and stopped in front of Danny and Isabelle. Towering over them, Melbourne glared down at Danny. He'd never felt so small and had the sudden urge to run away. Not that he'd have known where to run, of course, but with Isaac behind him and Melbourne in front, such a move was impossible. Instead, he just stood there and tried not to show he was... afraid? No, not afraid. Anxious perhaps. Nervous, certainly, but as he thought about it, he realised there really was no reason to be concerned. After all, without him, his friends—yes, he thought of them now as friends, would not have completed their quest.

'Step back, Melbourne,' commanded Ariadne. 'We need to see the Council of Elders. We have an urgent matter that needs to be discussed.'

Melbourne snorted and looked at Ariadne, studying her determined expression. Though she was a princess, Danny was surprised that Ariadne had the confidence to stand up to him like this. He was more than twice her size.

'Very well,' Melbourne said, turning to two centaur guards, waiting on his command. 'Call a council meeting,' he bellowed as the guards galloped out of the colosseum and towards the city.

This bizarre turn of events sent the crowd into a riot of intrigued murmurs. For some it was excitement, for others whispers of concern echoed around the stadium.

Melbourne escorted the group out of the colosseum and towards the city. Ariadne and Elda walked in front of him, looking far less confident than earlier, while Danny, Isabelle, Amir and Isaac cautiously followed behind. Professor Burmir hurried along next to them, doing his best to keep up on his short legs.

What began as a small entourage grew and grew, Arcadians spilling out from the colosseum to join the procession. Danny was nervous enough already and felt the last thing he needed was an audience. He wasn't sure what to expect from the council. They sounded important and Ariadne had said that they were 'all-knowing', which was intimidating enough. Danny just wanted to find out what had become of his father, and if he really was an Arcadian.

By the time they entered the city word of the strangers' presence had spread, and even more onlookers turned out to see what the fuss was about. It was safe to say that Danny had never seen such an interesting array of individuals. He saw nymphs selling their wares and Grigori children racing one another through the streets. A few centaurs were laughing at an unsuspecting Magi who had managed to set his coattails alight without noticing. Danny even saw a group of giants playing cards outside a tavern. The streets were alive with colour, but as they got closer to the palace, the streets grew quieter.

As they reached the palace gates, the impromptu crowd that had been following them dispersed.

Entering a vast courtyard, troops in military uniforms were going about their daily business. Some were guarding entrances to different parts of the palace. Others were marching as if practicing for an up-and-coming parade. It was impressive, but as Melbourne stopped at a large golden door, Danny shivered and reached out for Isabelle's hand. The domed roof cast an ominous shadow over the group.

'Wait here,' Melbourne commanded and walked through the door, leaving them alone in the courtyard.

'What happens now?' asked Danny, tired of following blindly.

'Melbourne will let the council know that we're here,' replied Amir, 'and then we go in and state our case.'

'Right,' sighed Danny nervously.

'Don't worry,' said Ariadne, sensing Danny's discomfort. 'The council is known for giving fair judgment and if you aren't Grigori, Arcadians have no power over mortals, so the worst they can do is send you home.'

That put Danny's mind to rest slightly. At least he couldn't be punished.

'What about you, though?' he asked Ariadne. 'Can you be punished for bringing me here?'

Amir looked at Ariadne, waiting to see if she was going to tell Danny the truth. She remained silent. 'Yes,' he said softly. 'We could be punished, and we'll face that problem if it arises, but Danny, we wouldn't have brought you here if we didn't believe it.'

'And let's face it,' said Elda, 'Isabelle's vision pretty much confirms it. We just need the council to make certain.'

'How do they do that?' asked Danny sceptically.

'Each of the tribe's Elders are on the council as well as two Magi Senators,' said Elda. 'They'll hear our case and decide on a verdict. If they think that you are Arcadian, they will ask our ancestors to confirm it.'

'Your ancestors?' asked Danny, clearly confused.

Before anyone could explain any further, Melbourne returned. 'You,' he said, pointing at Danny. 'Come with me.'

'What!' exclaimed Ariadne. 'Can't we go with him?'

'No, Princess,' replied Melbourne calmly. 'You've done enough, and he alone has been summoned.'

Danny looked forlornly at Ariadne. Why were they not allowed to come with him? He didn't want to go in alone, yet his feet started moving before his head had even decided to go. It was as if Melbourne's command had subconsciously convinced him to follow. Now he was scared. He turned back to look at the others as he stepped through the door. Why was he the only one to be summoned? What about Isabelle? What about the rest of his friends?

As Danny passed through the door, he gazed in awe around the room. The domed ceiling was as beautiful on the inside as out. The walls were lined with white marble columns and decorated with magnificent carvings. Sunbeams streamed in from floor to ceiling windows, casting light and cutting through the shadows, decorating the floor. The hall was spectacular, but the one overwhelming feature was the enormous tree that dominated the far end of the room. The thick trunk was covered in a thin layer of intricate gold lines, which pulsated and glistened in the light. They spread across the bark, reaching up to the ends of each branch. Danny noticed some of the lines fading to black and others that were glowing more brightly than the rest. On a raised platform in front of the tree stood a semi-circle of large throne-like chairs, decorated with carvings and inscriptions. Upon each chair sat an ominous figure dressed in ceremonial robes. They must be the eight Elders, Danny assumed. As he approached, he could feel their eyes watching him.

Ushered along by Melbourne, Danny walked slowly towards the Elders along a red velvet carpet that extended the length of the room. Elda had said that each council member represented a tribe and as he drew nearer, he could see golden plaques set on plinths at each of their sides. Each plaque was embossed with a unique symbol representing their tribe. Six of the Elders wore colourful robes with their tribe emblem embroidered into the chest. The other two Elders wore black robes with lightning-like flashes of red and orange and matching hats with tassels that spilled out from the top. From Elda's description, Danny guessed these two were the Magi Elders.

As the carpet came to an end at the base of the stairs, Melbourne gestured for Danny to stop. The tension in the room could be cut with a knife as one of the Elders, an elderly woman, stood up and looked down at him. Her plaque read 'Kelasso', matching the symbol on her robe. Her seat was one of two at the centre of the circle which, along with an emerald encrusted golden amulet on an equally elaborate chain of jewels, clearly showed her high status.

'You believe that you are one of us?' she addressed Danny.

Her voice was soft and lyrical while her eyes, although dark and intimidating, seemed to radiate kindness, something which Danny was grateful for given he could feel his whole body trembling. 'Don't be afraid,' she said, clearly noticing his discomfort. 'Please answer my question.'

'Yes,' he replied, trying to sound confident. 'Well, at least I think so.'

'And you travelled here from the mortal world with the young Prince and Princess?'

'Yes.' Danny nodded nervously.

'And why do they believe you are Arcadian?'

'Our friend, Isabelle, is a Seer. She had a vision of me wearing the Crown of Delos...'

'Impossible!' the representative from Delos exclaimed furiously as he rose from his seat—a pale man with piercing blue eyes glaring down at Danny. 'The Crown of Delos sits upon the head of King Lykos.'

Danny didn't know what to say, so he remained silent.

'Elias,' the Kelasso Elder shot him a look of stern distaste. 'If we are to place judgement on this boy's claim, then we must allow him to speak.'

Elias retook his seat reluctantly as Kelasso's Elder turned once more to Danny and nodded. 'Please continue.'

Danny wasn't sure what to say next. He didn't know what information would be most helpful, so instead, he decided to tell her everything. He spoke of the pirates kidnapping him on Isabelle's command. He told them of Xander's treasure and how his and Elda's 'hands of great power' had 'joined at the cave' to reveal the cave's treasure. He explained that his father was missing and that it was possible that he could be Adanion, son of Xander.

Up to this point the Elders had remained silent, patiently listening to his story, but when Danny spoke of Xander, the atmosphere changed. An air of tension, unnoticed by Danny, made the Elders shuffle in their seats.

Once he had finished telling his story, he looked up at the Elders, hoping beyond hope they would believe him. At first, they didn't move a muscle or say a word.

Each pair of eyes were fixed on him, studying him like a doctor might study a patient. Then as the Elders looked around at each other, they began to converse almost telepathically and with only the smallest of movements. The raising of an eyebrow here, the flicker of wrists there and the darting of eyes all seemed to add up to an entire conversation.

After only a few moments, but what for Danny felt like a lifetime, the Kelasso Elder broke the silence. 'Come here,' she said, beckoning him to approach her chair. 'I must verify your story.'

Danny had no idea how she was going to do that, but he did as he was told. He walked towards her, looking up at the other Elders who continued to study him closely. From here, he could see in greater detail the intricate patterns on the tree. They seemed to flow like liquid rivers of gold and black forming tributaries that wound in and out of each other as they spread up the trunk and disappeared into the canopy. It was beautiful and truly mesmerising. The entire surface of the tree simply rippled with colour as if it were alive.

The woman reached down and offered up her palm. Her hands were long and bony, and her fingernails were like colourful steel daggers. Warily, Danny reached out and she took his hand in hers.

Closing her eyes, Danny instantly felt a jolt of static that shot up his arm, engulfing his entire body in a tingling sensation of euphoria. His pupils dilated and he felt his mind replaying memories of days gone by, but also some of which he had no recollection.

When she let go of his hand, he felt like he was in shock, his mind having been picked apart in the finest of detail. He looked up at the woman who stared back at him, an intrigued expression on her wrinkled face. Without a word, she turned and walked back towards the tree. She reached out and, with one of her rough, bony fingers, traced the glowing lines with her fingernail. There was silence across the room as the other Elders watched her work. She dragged her nail back and forth following the flows of gold and black until, at last, she pressed her other hand hard against the trunk as if she were trying to reach deep within them… Opening her eyes suddenly, she stopped.

'Here,' she announced. 'I've found him.'

Her fingernail was hovering above one of the black lines. Danny had no clue what this meant. What did 'I've found him' mean? He couldn't wrap his head around it.

She turned and faced Danny once more. 'Come to me,' she commanded.

Danny climbed the steps and slowly walked towards her. Passing between two of the thrones he was only too aware of the Elders eyes watching his every move as he joined the Kelasso Elder and stood by her side.

'Here,' she said, pointing to a thin black line on the trunk of the tree. 'Place your hand here.'

Danny reached out towards the tree. At first, he felt a tingling sensation emanating from the bark and then, as he touched the black line with the tip of his finger, it turned from black to gold and like a liquid bolt of lightning shot up from the earth to the sky. It shone like a beacon through the canopy and engulfed the room in a golden glow. The light faded away and the tingling sensation left Danny's body.

He jumped back in shock as the Elders immediately turned to each other, this time dispensing with any form of telepathy or secret communication and whispering frantically among themselves.

'Could he really be Xander's son?' one said, an old man whose long white beard brushed along the floor as he stood up and turned to his neighbour.

'Is he definitely from Delos?' chimed in another, a dark haired Elder whose feline features intrigued Danny as he followed the voices around the room.

'What does this mean for King Lykos?' another questioned, looking towards Elias.

Elias appeared unnerved and kept a calm expression on his face, but his fists were balled tightly in his lap, clearly showing his disapproval of Danny and the suggestions surrounding his lineage.

Danny was more confused than ever and looked to the Kelasso Elder who, unlike her other Council members, remained calm.

'You *are* one of us,' she told him with a smile and a graceful bow of her head. She then turned to the other Elders who were still bickering amongst themselves.

'I have looked into this boy's mind,' she said, her voice commanding the room, 'and the tree of ancestors has spoken. I can confirm this child is the son of Alexander Blake.'

The council erupted with questions once more, but they were

quickly silenced with a raise of the Kelasso Elder's hand. 'We have all heard the rumours surrounding Alexander Blake,' she continued, 'and now that this boy is safely within the walls of Osaria, I must reveal the true story to you all.'

'I have been the leader of this council for almost twenty years,' she began. 'And only now is it safe to reveal this well-kept secret. Seventeen years ago, when the old Delos King, Ezikeiel died, his sister Leonora was set to inherit the throne. The story as you know it was that Leonora was kidnapped by Alexander and taken into hiding. By the time the Delos army found them, he had fled, and she had been murdered. From that day forth, he has been considered an outlaw but...' She paused 'This story is a lie, a lie spread far and wide by Delos's current king, Lykos.'

'Outrageous!' bellowed Elias as he jumped up from his chair, his voice so loud Danny was convinced his friends outside would be able to hear.

Kelesso's Elder ignored this interruption and continued speaking. 'King Lykos wanted the throne more than anything else. Being the third born, he was not entitled to it. Leonora knew that her younger brother would stop at nothing to claim what he considered to be his birth right and she knew his corrupted followers would help him. So, after Lykos murdered Ezekiel…' Cries of disbelief echoed around the room. 'He tried to murder Leonora, too. Alexander, who was in love with Leonora, whisked her away to safety. They took with them the Crown of Delos in hopes that its political weight may gain them safe passage. In the months they were gone, Lykos took control of Delos and began to search for his sister. In so doing, he made it clear that his hopes were to find her and restore her to the throne, but Lykos had a darker intention. When he found Leonora, he planned to kill her. And that is exactly what he did.

'There was however, one thing he did not account for, Leonora and Alexander had conceived a child. A son, by the name of Adanion. When Lykos found them, he killed poor Leonora, and Xander could do nothing but take the child and the Crown of Delos and flee. Lykos searched high and low for them. He even sent Reapers after them, but they had vanished. Alexander took Adanion to the mortal world and there he stayed to raise his son away from their bloodthirsty family.'

'You're making up this ridiculous tale. How could you possibly know this?' cried Elias, standing up in rage.

She turned and glared at this latest interruption. Elias returned to his seat.

'Before he left Arcadia,' she continued, 'Alexander visited me in my home in Kelasso. He told me of the treachery afoot and made me promise to keep his secret until a time came when it was safe to reveal Adanion's true identity and restore him to the throne. I believe it is fate that brought you here, Adanion.' She looked at Danny.

'This can't be true!' shouted Elias, this time not to be ignored. 'Delos will not stand for these lies.'

'Be quiet, Elias!' she commanded, her voice seeming to bounce off the walls. 'I suggest you be very careful before you accuse me of being a liar. I have seen into his mind and the ancestor tree has ignited his Arcadian lifeline.'

As the remainder of the Elders looked towards Elias, he stood and reached into his robe. Producing an orb, he raised it in the air, crushed it in his hand and disappeared through the portal.

The room was left in a state of shock and the realisation that the consequences of this information would be life-changing sunk in. More and more discussion ensued among the remaining Elders. Many lives would be changed, and many paths altered, especially if they planned to overthrow Lykos.

Melbourne stepped forward and placed a hand on Danny's shoulder. Danny knew that Melbourne had meant to comfort him but, having just heard life-altering news and been given very vague details about his future, the hand felt like just another weight on his shoulder. All they could do at this moment was wait for instructions. It was far too much for Danny to process.

EPILOGUE

The next morning Danny woke, still in a daze, and slowly sat up in his bed. He looked around the room, a grand but simple design, with light blue walls and tall windows that let in plenty of light. He had no idea how he'd got there, but according to Ariadne who sat on the end of his bed, he'd fainted and was carried home by Melbourne.

'What do you mean, I fainted?' objected Danny. 'I've never fainted in my life.'

'Well, you did this time,' grinned Ariadne. 'And to be fair, it's hardly surprising given what you went through.'

'Where am I?' he asked, hoping to change the subject.

'You're in the palace,' said Elda, who sat on a chair at the end of the bed.

'The palace,' he spluttered. 'What on earth am I doing here?'

'You belong here, Danny,' said Ariadne. 'I know it's hard to understand, but you are part of the Royal family.'

'Is he awake?' asked Isaac as he came in from the balcony, followed by Amir.

'He's just woken up,' said Ariadne.

'And he's a bit confused,' chuckled Elda.

Danny looked round at his friends. 'Royal family? Did I really faint?'

'Yep!' laughed Isaac.

'The Elders, they…' Danny began to say.

'We've been told what happened,' Amir smiled. 'Didn't expect you to be Royalty too, but at least you've found your family.'

Danny thought about this for a minute. He now knew who his parents were, which was amazing. He had wondered about his father for years but knowing who they were wasn't the same as knowing them. It was confirmed that his mother was dead. He felt sad about this, of course, but he hadn't ever known her, which made it hard to be upset. He still had no idea where his father was, or even if he was alive. So much new information was circling around his head, and he was finding it hard to process. He didn't expect his mother to be royalty, a piece of information he was glad he now knew, but what did it mean for his future? Finding out that he was a Prince was as vague a concept to him as being Grigori. He had more questions now than ever before.

He looked at his friends as they gathered around his bed. 'What happens now?' he asked.

'Isabelle's being questioned by the Elders,' said Elda. 'Apparently she's one of the strongest Seers they've ever encountered. They've sent a team out into the mortal world to search for her sister, but as only Moreno knew where she was hidden, we've no idea how long that might take, even if they're able to find her at all.'

'I hope they find her,' said Danny.

'They will, it's just a matter of time,' continued Elda. 'As for us, we aren't facing any punishment at all. We're actually being praised for bringing you back with us. King Cyrus has planned a homecoming feast for all the returning teams and wants you to join us.'

'And as for Selena...,' said Ariadne.

'Selena?' asked Danny.

'Darius' shady wife,' she reminded him. 'She's being questioned about the secret meeting I saw her having with the horseman who dropped the gold coin. She's definitely involved somehow. We're not sure yet how it all fits together but without it we may never have found the treasure.'

'Which is set to be retrieved!' chipped in Isaac excitedly.

'Great' laughed Danny. 'That should be interesting. I wonder what else they'll find in that cavern.'

'You'll find out soon enough,' said Ariadne. 'Elda's been asked to lead a team back there for the excavation.' Elda looked very excited and pleased from her perch at the foot of the bed.

'What about Delos?' asked Danny, realising that they wouldn't simply accept his presence in Arcadia.

'All of their dignitaries have either left court or are acting really suspiciously. We don't know what's going to come from your presence here, but one thing's for sure, Delos is worried.'

'They should be,' said Elda. 'Danny, I'm not sure if you've quite realised this yet, but you are the true heir to the throne of Delos.'

The news of a new family, a new species, a new realm and finding out that he was the rightful king of Delos was... well, overwhelming, but Danny was just, more than anything, excited for his next adventure.

The others watched as he got out of bed and walked out onto the balcony. He stood looking out over the city. The sun was setting over the desert as Ariadne, Elda, Isaac and Amir joined him. Standing alongside his friends, he felt at peace as he watched the dark red sun of the Arcadian kingdom disappear over the horizon. He wondered what his new life might bring, what dangers or adventures he might face in the future... But at that moment, he didn't care what the coming days would bring. He looked at his friends, thinking just how lucky he was to have finally found his family.

To be continued...

ACKNOWLEDGEMENTS

EDITOR

Anthony Turner

ILLUSTRATOR

Almay Beukman

PROOFREADER

Sophie Deakin

This book wouldn't have become a reality without your help, thank you so much for your time and your hard work. Anthony, I cannot thank you enough for your contribution to this project. Your advice and guidance have been crucial, and your reality checks have saved me more than once.

Thank you.